*The Wilderness Walk*

SHEILA BISHOP

# *The Wilderness Walk*

**HURST & BLACKETT**

HURST & BLACKETT LTD
*3 Fitzroy Square, London W1*

AN IMPRINT OF THE  HUTCHINSON GROUP

London Melbourne Sydney Auckland
Wellington Johannesburg Cape Town
and agencies throughout the world

*First published 1972*

*This book has been set in Garamond type, printed in
Great Britain by Anchor Press, and bound
by Wm. Brendon, both of Tiptree, Essex*

ISBN 0 09 110010 0

# I

Nearly all the houses surrounding Lincoln's Inn Fields were occupied by lawyers. Arthur Reed lived on the eastern side of the square with his wife Lavinia, their four children, and Lavinia's unmarried sister Caroline Prior. The dark rooms on the ground floor were filled with heavy furniture, law books, and clerks on high stools industriously copying briefs. After dinner, when the clerks had gone home, Mr. Reed often returned to his chambers to browse through the work of the day and contemplate his responsibilities, for he was a serious-minded man who enjoyed feeling useful.

He was also a conscientious husband and as soon as he heard the rattle of the tea-tray on the landing overhead he always went upstairs to join his wife and sister-in-law in the drawing-room.

It was a high, narrow room, charmingly furnished. Lavinia's taste certainly did him credit, he thought for the hundredth time, one June evening in 1816, as he came bustling in with a smile on his rather solemn face, for he had a piece of good news, a delightful surprise which he had been saving up for this moment.

Lavinia was at the tea-table. She was a beautiful creature, slender and graceful, with her white neck and shoulders, her classic profile, and her mass of fine, fair hair which someone had once described as the colour of moonlight.

Her eyes were a soft violet blue. She was twenty-nine years old and looked a great deal younger.

Caroline Prior, though a passable-looking young woman, could not compare with her sister. Her hair and skin were rather brown, and her nose was too prominent. But she was intelligent and seemed to find a good deal in life to laugh at (a fact which sometimes puzzled her relations) and she had a very pleasing figure. She was standing by the long window, gazing down into the square, which had acquired a kind of strangeness with the shadowy half-tones of dusk.

Arthur was a little put out by the sight of the naked windows. 'Why has not Boulter pulled the curtains?' he demanded.

'I told her to leave them,' replied his wife. 'There was such a pretty sunset.'

'But my dear girl, people can see in.'

'Does it matter? We weren't doing anything we shouldn't.'

'I should hope not. That is hardly the point.' Arthur realised just in time that if he started scolding Lavinia now it would spoil the effect of his surprise. He deftly changed the subject, saying: 'I am sure there are better places for admiring a sunset than Lincoln's Inn. I am only sorry that you are not able to pay your usual visit to Buckinghamshire this year, but my mother's state of health makes it quite ineligible for her to have the children at Holdsworth . . .'

'Yes, Arthur, I know. It is out of the question.'

'However, I have made another arrangement. How would you like to spend a corple of months by the sea?'

'At Ramsgate, you mean? Or Worthing?'

'No, the children are too young for such a place, it would

6

not suit. The seaside holidays of your own childhood were very different, and I know what happy memories you have of Martland Farm. In short, I have been corresponding with Mrs. Duffet, and you are to go there next week.'

He achieved his surprise. Lavinia stared at him, absolutely thunderstruck. 'You have arranged for me to go back to Cleave?'

'You and Caroline and the children—and Nurse, of course. It will be a long, expensive journey, but I know it will give you so much pleasure. You are pleased, aren't you, my love?' he asked with an unusual touch of doubt.

'Oh yes, Arthur—certainly. How—how clever of you to think of such a splendid plan!'

He was instantly reassured, glad to feel that she was just as grateful as she ought to be. He was luckily unaware of Caroline's raised eyebrows and ironic expression. They would have annoyed him.

Caroline had lived with the Reeds for ten years; she was pretty well used to their foibles by now, and knew when to venture tactfully into the conversation and when to keep her mouth shut. She came across to the table, enquiring how Arthur had made these arrangements for surely he himself had never been to Cleave?

'I wrote to that old friend of your mother's, Mrs. Harper: I asked her whether the same family was still at Martland Farm, and hearing that they continue to let lodgings I felt no hesitation in applying to them. Mrs. Duffet assures me that you will have the same parlour you always had in the old days, and she will engage an extra maidservant to wait on you. I am sure you will be very snug and I mean to come down to join you as soon as the term is over.'

He went on talking in this way until it was time to go

to bed, not noticing that most of the questions and comments came from Caroline; Lavinia said very little.

Caroline was far more conscious of what was going on in her sister's mind, and when she retreated into her own bedroom and shut the door she knew that she would soon have a visitor. Sure enough, she had hardly taken off her dress when Lavinia came running in, breathless and agitated.

'Caro, you must help me! What are we to do?'

'To escape the necessity of going to Cleave? You will have to tell Arthur how much you dislike the prospect; I can see no other way.'

'You know I can't do that.'

'Why not? Surely he must be aware of the painful associations—that we were down there when Papa lost all his money?'

'I think it may have slipped his memory, and I cannot possibly remind him, after he has taken so much trouble. You know how upset he gets when people don't fall in with his plans.'

Caroline thought that Lavinia was far too subservient to her husband's wishes, but she was unable to say so, knowing that this was partly due to Lavinia's deep sense of obligation, and that she herself was one of the items Lavinia had to be obliged about. It was not every man who would marry a penniless wife, and then take on the burden of her equally penniless mother and sister. That was what Arthur Reed had done.

'Well then, we shall have to make the best of things,' she said. 'Shall you mind so very much?'

'Of course I shall mind. Don't you understand, Caro? If we go back to Cleave, it may be impossible to avoid—I shall probably have to meet that man!'

8

'If you mean Francis Aubrey,' said Caroline, irritated by her sister's histrionics, 'you might as well say so. You can hardly have forgotten his name.'

Lavinia said in a trembling voice that Caroline had no sensibility. She did not appreciate the misery and humiliation caused by a broken engagement.

'I'm sure it was very disagreeable, but it all happened a long while ago, and you were well rid of Lord Francis.'

'You always disliked him.'

'He made me think of Richard III.'

'He wasn't a hunchback,' said Lavinia, affronted. She would never have accepted a proposal from a man who was actually deformed.

'He was small and ugly, and there was something uncomfortable about him. We were never easy when he was there. You only said you'd marry him because Mama encouraged you, and he was the brother of a marquess.'

'I did not care for him as I ought,' admitted Lavinia. 'I should never have agreed to an engagement. I was flattered, and I did not know then what he was like. By the end, I was most dreadfully afraid of him. He is wicked and cruel.'

Good heavens, thought Caroline, what can the monster have done to her?

'I could not bear to see him again,' faltered Lavinia. 'What are we to do? I wish you would think of something, Caro.'

'I'll do my best,' said Caroline, without much conviction.

Seated in front of the looking-glass, after Lavinia had gone, she began to brush her thick, soft hair, casting back her mind to her childhood and those early visits to Cleave.

She was five years younger than Lavinia, and they were the only surviving children of a man who had once been a wealthy banker. They had lived in a very grand style in Curzon Street; their parents had entertained prodigally and been invited everywhere. But every summer Mrs. Prior retired from town life and took her two young daughters to stay at a quiet farmhouse she had discovered near Cleave in South Devon. Cleave was not a proper watering-place, it was simply a fishing village that had been improved. There was one fair-sized house in the parish: Hoyle Park, which belonged to the Marquess of Eltham, though it was not his principal seat, which was at Dillingford in Kent.

Mrs. Prior and her daughters had gone to Martland Farm as usual in the summer of 1804. Lavinia was just seventeen, no longer a child, but a young lady who had come out into the world. They found that the Aubrey family were in residence at Hoyle Park: the widowed Lady Eltham and her children, including the young Marquess, a boy of about Caroline's age, who had been left in the guardianship of his uncle, Lord Francis Aubrey. He too was staying at the Park.

A younger son with expensive tastes, Lord Francis made a dead set at the heiress. Caroline, at twelve, was an uncompromising romantic; she was shocked to see her beautiful sister encouraging the morose little man she would not have looked at twice if he wasn't a lord. Naturally no one consulted Caroline. Lord Francis proposed, Lavinia accepted him, and there was much congratulating and celebrating—interrupted by a desperate and incoherent letter from Mr. Prior in London, announcing that the bank had failed.

Caroline paused, hand in mid-air, gazing at her own image in the glass. Fronds of hair, vigorously brushed and combed, came floating upwards of their own volition.

She hated to remember the time that followed. It had

been the collapse of their world. Their whole outlook on the future had changed, nearly all their material possessions had been swept away. Worst of all, she had realised that her parents were quite overwhelmed and bewildered. Lavinia's engagement was one of the ruins. As soon as she knew that her father had lost all his money, she made the traditional gesture—she wrote to Lord Francis and offered to release him. Any man of honour would have stuck to his promise, but this scion of the nobility had seized his chance to escape. He did not want Lavinia without her fortune. And whatever they might pretend now, this had been a bitter blow at the time. Lavinia had cried dreadfully: she did not know what was going to become of her.

The Priors had struggled along for the next year in poky lodgings at Edgware, and there Mr. Prior had died. (Caroline had never been certain whether his long and fatal illness had been the cause of the disaster or its result.) His lawyers had gone on trying to recover some of the loans he had made to various former clients. One of these lawyers was Arthur Reed, who fell in love with Lavinia and was determined to marry her. Arthur was not exactly a romantic figure, but he was tall and reasonably well-looking in a solid sort of way—certainly a great deal handsomer than Francis Aubrey. And besides, handsome is as handsome does, and his chivalrous desire to take care of Lavinia and her family was a very pleasant contrast to the treatment she had received from Lord Francis.

After the wedding Mrs. Prior and Caroline had come to live with the Reeds. Mrs. Prior had sunk into a premature invalidism and died in 1813. Lavinia's marriage had turned out fairly happily. She and Arthur were genuinely devoted, though it seemed strange to Caroline how often they managed to distress and irritate each other without ever knowing why. This affair of the seaside holiday was a case in point. Arthur had never considered whether his wife would want to go back to a place which would revive so much of the past, and as she was apparently unable to discuss the matter with him, he would probably end by being hurt and disappointed at her lack of enthusiasm.

Caroline went to bed with her head full of Lavinia's problems, and after a night's sleep she woke with at least one good idea.

As soon as Arthur had eaten his breakfast and gone downstairs, she asked her sister, 'How much would you dislike going to Devonshire if you were sure there was no danger of meeting Francis Aubrey?'

'I should not mind at all—it is the dread of an encounter hanging over one—for how can we possibly tell if he will be there or not?'

'Well, I have been thinking: Jack Eltham is a grown man by now, past the age of needing a guardian, so his uncle may not be so much in evidence. I thought I might pay a morning-call at Eltham House and see what I can find out.'

'Call on Lady Eltham! You can't possibly do such a thing. You know we don't move in those circles now. And besides, she hasn't seen you since you were a child, she would think you either very encroaching or quite mad.'

'So she would if she was there? Isn't it lucky she is in Scotland?'

'How do you know?'

'I read a piece of silly chat about her in the newspaper. One of the daughters (Lady Lucy, I think) is married to a Scotsman and expecting to be confined, and her mother has gone up there for the great event.'

'But if the Marchioness is not at home, how will you find out about Francis?'

'I shall pump the servants.'

Lavinia gave a bleat of dismay. How could Caro be so vulgar? And how was she to get all the way to Eltham House? She could not possibly go in a hackney carriage . . .

'Certainly not. I shall walk.'

'You can't walk all that distance, you will be quite done-up. And it would be very improper. I suppose I could send Patience with you . . .'

'A fine figure of fun I should cut in Berkeley Square, with dear old Patience plodding along behind me on her bunions! Stop croaking, my love; I am well able to take care of myself.'

She set off cheerfully, ten minutes later, prepared to enjoy her little adventure. She liked walking and was not at all nervous, unlike Lavinia. She crossed Lincoln's Inn Fields; there were a lot of children playing in the gardens, including her niece Vinny and her nephew Ben. The way to Mayfair lay along High Holborn, a respectable street which ran through one of the poorest districts in London, so the people in their workaday clothes were inclined to be shabby, and Caroline felt a little conspicuous in the white muslin dress she had put on to impress Lord Eltham's butler. Presently she came to the jostle of Oxford Street, and at last reached the familiar left-hand turn into New Bond Street. Here the atmosphere was entirely different. No one apparently had any work to do, everyone was sauntering along in the sunshine, and practically all the saunterers were people of fashion. Caroline was pleased to note that most of the younger ladies were dressed in white. She lingered for a little in front of the tempting shop windows of milliners, perfumiers and music-sellers, but soon turned off again into the maze of quiet streets and squares that lay in the angle between Piccadilly and Park Lane.

Eltham House was one of those mansions that stood in splendid isolation behind its own railings, with all the dignity of a short carriage-sweep and a lofty portico. Caroline was not easily over-awed. She walked smartly up to the front door and rang the bell.

Her ring was answered by a footman who looked as though he had only just shrugged himself into his livery jacket. He was quite young and had not yet learnt to be supercilious. Caroline asked for Lady Eltham.

'I regret, madam, her ladyship is out of town.'

'Oh dear. I suppose she is still in Scotland, with Lady Lucy?'

The footman admitted that this was so.

'I wonder, can you tell me, whether the family are likely to be down at Hoyle Park this summer?'

She was so obviously a well-brought-up young lady, and spoke so unaffectedly, that the footman had no hesitation in answering. 'I fancy there is no talk of opening the house at Cleave this year.'

She thanked him for the information, which was exactly what she had hoped for, and quickly turned away before he had time to ask for her card.

As she reached the railings, she met two people who were just coming in : a tall and decidedly handsome young man in a blue swallow-tail coat, light pantaloons and hessian boots, accompanied by an exquisite little sylph of a girl, not more than eighteen years old, with large, pansy-velvet eyes, a dazzling complexion, a much be-feathered hat, and a low-cut dress that fitted her like a stocking. They stood aside to let Caroline pass, and the young man took off his hat and made her a slight bow.

Why, she thought, as she walked briskly away, I believe that was Lord Eltham. And I suppose that dashing girl is what they call a cyprian. He certainly looks quite emancipated from the supervision of a guardian.

## 2

'Who was that, just leaving the house as we arrived, Thomas?' enquired Jack Eltham, handing his hat to the footman.

'A caller who came to ask for her ladyship, my lord. I did not ascertain her name.'

'Acquainted with my mother, was she? Oh well, it can't be helped,' said the young man, glancing at his companion; her situation in life was perfectly obvious, and the footman saw exactly what his employer meant. Knowing his place, he said nothing and looked particularly wooden.

'You have a very imposing house, Eltham,' said the velvet-eyed girl, gazing through the glass doors of the vestibule at the marble staircase.

'A little too like St. Paul's Cathedral for my taste. I've only come home to read my letters. Will you fetch them for me, if you please?' he added to Thomas.

'Very good, my lord.'

Jack led the way into a room that opened off the hall.

'Come in here, Ada.'

Ada Gainey considered the small saloon dreadfully old-fashioned; it was full of mirrors heavily framed in acanthus leaves, and gilt chairs with curly legs. There was a picture of a lady in a wig who looked a perfect fright, though of course it wouldn't do to say so.

'What a beautiful room,' she remarked politely.

Jack came up behind her and removed her hat. Her dark hair was cut quite short. He began to kiss the back of her neck. She endured this passively for a moment, and then said, 'Don't, Eltham,' in a cool little voice.

'What's the matter?'

'I don't want to be pulled about.'

'There's something more than that. What is it?'

She hedged and disclaimed; there was nothing at all the matter, nothing to signify—eventually it came out.

'My sister Hester keeps saying you ought to rent a house for me. She says the Marquess of Eltham ought to provide a better setting for the triumph of Eros than someone else's back bedroom.'

'Oh, does she?' said Jack, scowling.

'My sisters are forever saying you treat me like a common opera-girl, and my mother wonders why you don't make me a settlement. The others have houses and settlements (except for Sally who is always so unfortunate) and last year Tom Oatley took me to Brighton, but now I am forced to live in Mount Street with my parents, and my mother is often very unkind . . .'

'My poor little love, I can't bear to think of you being unhappy. You shall have your house, I promise.'

'Shall I, Jack? How soon?'

The acquisitive note in her voice seemed to him as innocent as the calculation of a child wheedling sweets. He kissed her gently, and said: 'As soon as I come to terms with my uncle. I have written to tell him that I need a larger allowance.'

'What's it to do with him? You are over twenty-one.'

'My father left a damnably stupid will. Everything is tied up until I marry. He appointed his brother to act as my trustee.'

'But that's absurd. Suppose you were to remain a bachelor all your life?'

'It was a mistake, of course. A conditional clause about my age had been left out. But you try to get my uncle to agree . . .'

Ada listened and sympathised and stored up the facts, wondering if she could turn them to her own advantage. She had been taught to think in this way. She was the youngest of a family of five beautiful girls, all of whom had been launched into the London demi-monde as cyprians, courtesans of the most exclusive sort who accepted lovers only from the aristocracy. The Golden Gaineys were as Famous as the Dubochet girls—Harriette Wilson and her sisters. Their nickname was an allusion to their colouring (all the sisters had light red hair, except Ada) but there was a double meaning: the suggestion of gain and gold was certainly appropriate.

The butler came in, bringing a pile of letters on a salver. Jack glanced quickly through them.

'Has there been nothing delivered by hand? From Lord Francis?'

'No, my lord.'

'Has he not written? What shall you do?' asked Ada.

'Take you for a drive in the park.'

They passed the next few hours very pleasantly, but Jack had not forgotten this conversation, and at four o'clock, having deposited Ada with her favourite sister Betsey, he drove along Piccadilly to call on his uncle, who had a set of chambers in Albany.

Melbourne House, once the focus of Whig society, had

later passed to the Duke of York, who relinquished it in a cloud of debt; now, with a new name and a great deal of alteration and additional building, it had become a unique apartment house for gentlemen of means. Jack was admitted by the porter, and made his way to Lord Francis Aubrey's chambers on the first floor of the original mansion. A peaceful, almost reverent silence reigned inside Albany—there were stringent rules about noise. Many of the rooms had been chopped about and sub-divided; Lord Francis leased a small bedroom and a kitchen, as well as accommodation for his servant in the attic and his wine in the cellar, but the glory of his apartment was a great room looking over Burlington Gardens, crammed with so many brilliantly coloured porcelain ornaments that they always made Jack blink, though he knew what to expect. His uncle was an impassioned collector of *chinoiserie.*

All along the walls there were cabinets filled with his treasures, which also occupied two shelved alcoves, as well as part of a bookcase, the books having been taken out and stacked on the floor. Some of the vases were plump and round, others were slender, with long graceful necks. Most of them were decorated with floral designs: delicate peonies and carnations against a black ground, dazzling white sprays on a surface of lustrous blue. Jack began to wander round the room, inspecting the pieces more closely. There was a plate sprawling with golden dragons which took his fancy, and several pairs of china birds, recognisably pheasants, ducks and geese, but he thought the plumage was too exotic to be copied from life. He picked up one of the pheasants.

'For God's sake put that down before you drop it!' said a voice behind his left shoulder.

Lord Francis Aubrey had come into the room quite

silently, which was one of his disagreeable habits. He was about forty years old, short and spare, with cropped brown hair and rather pale skin. His features were quite undistinguished, though there was a hint of cynical intelligence in his light grey eyes. He gave the impression of a selfish and perhaps ruthless man who travelled his own road, unhampered by social graces. He looked his nephew over, and said, 'What do you want?'

'I thought I would just look in,' said Jack, in what he hoped was a nonchalant manner. He had safely restored the pheasant; his eye fell on the pot standing next to it. 'That's a nice bright red.'

'*Sang de bœuf.*'

'Oh?'

'Bull's blood,' Lord Francis kindly translated.

'Thank you, sir. I do understand French.'

'Of course. It was Latin that floored you at Eton, wasn't it?'

I won't let him rile me, thought Jack.

'You aren't likely to get any more money out of me, my dear Eltham, by coming here and making ill-informed remarks about oriental porcelain.'

'Very well, sir,' said Jack, flushing. 'If you prefer to come straight to the point. May I know whether you intend to increase my allowance?'

'Not at present.'

'Oh, look here, sir—this is quite unreasonable! Why won't you give me a proper income? I'm entitled to keep up my position. I need the money...'

'To throw into the lap of one of the most mercenary young women in London.'

Jack had not realised that his uncle knew of his liaison with Ada, but he came back with a quick rejoinder.

'You've no right to abuse her. You've never even met her.'

'I've met her sisters. They're all birds of a feather.'

'Hester Gainey used to be your mistress, so I can't see what right you have to disapprove . . .'

'I don't disapprove. I am not a moralist.'

'Oh.' Jack was slightly put out. It was not the sort of answer you expected from a member of the older generation, even Uncle Francis.

'I think you are somewhat confused,' said his uncle. 'I am no longer your guardian, merely your trustee. Therefore I need not object to your having a mistress, I simply object to your having a very expensive mistress.'

'I cannot be mean about falling in love.'

'Then you will have to make your economies elsewhere.'

'You don't appear to make many economies yourself, sir.'

Lord Francis looked round complacently at his collection. 'Surely you do not grudge me my modest pleasures?'

Jack had an obscure feeling that if he, the head of the family, had to make economies, then the pleasures of a younger son ought to be a good deal more modest than they appeared. He was too well-bred to say so.

It was all the fault of that absurd will. His uncle was able to keep him tied to an allowance which had no relation, as far as he could see, to his actual income. If he doesn't take care, thought Jack, I shall go out and get married to the first girl I see, and it will serve him right.

There was one way in which his uncle could not thwart him. Although his income was so restricted, Jack had the right to live in any of his different houses and to make full use of his material possessions.

20

'I shall take Ada down to Devonshire,' he announced. 'You can't prevent me going to Hoyle. If she wants a house of her own, she shall have the cottage in the Wilderness.'

## 3

'But I don't want to go and be buried in the country,' protested Ada. 'I hate the country. There's nothing to do and it always rains.'

'You'll do what you're told, my girl, and listen to those who know what's best for you!' exclaimed the big, red-faced woman who was standing over her in a threatening attitude.

Ada began to cry.

'Be careful, Mama. You know how easily she bruises,' said her sister Betsey. 'Can't you let her alone? Why should she go if she doesn't want to?'

'Because it would be madness to throw away such a magnificent prospect,' retorted Hester, the eldest and most successful of the five Gainey daughters. 'Tell us again, Ada. What was it exactly that Lord Eltham said to you about getting married?'

A family conference was taking place at the house in Mount Street where Mr. and Mrs. Gainey had lived precariously for many years and then in growing prosperity.

If Martha Gainey had heard herself described as a bawd who had grown rich on the prostitution of her own daughters, she would have been highly indignant. She loved her girls, all she cared for was their advancement. She was the child of a housemaid and (perhaps) a gentleman. After a short spell on the stage she had married an unsuccessful artist. Her personal life had been unhappy, but she had produced five celestially beautiful children. For their sake she had stuck to her husband, who made a little money teaching; she had scrimped and squeezed and taken in lodgers, and every penny she could get was spent on lessons and accomplishments for the girls, who were being brought up to make good marriages. At that time she had no other end in view.

When Hester was seduced at fifteen, her outraged mother thrashed her with a broom-handle and locked her in the attic on a diet of bread and water. No parent could have done more to show her disapproval. Shortly afterwards Hester ran away, and when next seen she was the proud tenant of a villa at Richmond, with a smart phaeton and a pearl necklace, all the most delightful wages of sin. Mrs. Gainey could not bear to be estranged from her favourite child, and it had also begun to dawn on her that her daydreams had misfired. The girls were becoming so accomplished that they would be wasted on the sort of men who were likely to marry them. If they dispensed with marriage, however, they could lead interesting, luxurious lives with partners who would be worthy of their great beauty. That was how it had all begun.

So here, at thirty-four, was Hester, still the pick of the bunch, with her red-gold hair and her green eyes: the official mistress of a wealthy Member of Parliament, she entertained princes and poets, and managed to keep on the right side of innumerable lovers with extraordinary poise and diplomacy. Sally, the second sister, had not done so well for herself. Poor Sally, she was so unfortunate, always falling in love with scoundrels or having babies at the wrong moment. She sat in the window, watching Ada, her large eyes filled with tears of sympathy.

The third sister, Celia, was missing. She had actually married one of her protectors and was now the Honourable Mrs. Page; she did not come to see her mother very often. Celia had always been a quiet, refined girl, unlike lively Betsey, with her brazen head and her quick tongue. Betsey was twenty-two, four years older than Ada, and at present the mistress of a dashing Hussar.

The one remaining member of the family was absent, but no one missed him. Mr. Gainey was usually drunk by dinner-time, and he had never counted for much in that matriarchal household.

'Come along, Ada,' prompted her mother. 'What did Eltham say?'

'He promised I should have a house of my own—that was yesterday morning—and then when he came to see me at Betsey's last night, he said it was just some horrid cottage on his estate in Devonshire, which I thought was downright shabby. Who wants a house in Devonshire?'

'But what did he say about getting married? Did he make you an offer?'

'No, of course not. Did he, Bets?'

'Not precisely,' admitted Betsey. 'He said he would be driven into matrimony in order to get possession of his own fortune. And then he said that the day would come when he would be able to cover Ada in diamonds from head to toe. You could hardly call that a declaration. Corbet was there too and he said Eltham wasn't serious.'

'Not about covering Ada in diamonds,' said Hester. 'But I dare say he is perfectly serious in his desire to end the deadlock over his inheritance. I suppose he might go through a marriage of convenience with some well-bred

23

little nonentity, but somehow I don't think he will. He's one of those young romantics, I don't believe he will bring himself to propose to one woman while his heart is set on another. And that is your great chance, Ada. If his passion for you and his determination to marry go on increasing about equally, then he will end by making you his wife.'

Ada seemed quite dazed by this prophecy, she stood gaping at Hester with her mouth open.

'I wonder whether such a brilliant match has much hope of felicity,' said Sally anxiously. 'Lord Eltham's friends won't like it, and I dare say they might treat Ada very un-kindly. And she will be lost to us, I fear. I believe Celia's husband has forbidden her to come near us.'

'Hold your tongue, you stupid hen,' snapped her mother, casting a wary eye at Ada. 'Celia don't come here any more because she's ashamed of us. Ada's not so poor-spirited. Are you, my pet?'

'No, Mama. How long do you think it will take Eltham to make up his mind?'

'A month or two, maybe,' said Hester. 'I am very glad, as it turns out, that he has suggested taking you out of town, for once you are alone together in the peace of the countryside, I am sure his attachment will become even stronger. There will be nothing else for him to think about. Let me give you a word of advice, by the way . . .'

'Don't get into low company,' said Betsey, rolling her eyes.

'Certainly not. But she mustn't try to get into good society either. Do you understand me, Ada? Once you are married to a man of Eltham's consequence you will be accepted everywhere. Even though your past is an open secret, the nobility and gentry are such a pack of hypocrites that they will be able to pretend ignorance—provided they have been spared the embarrassment of meeting you before the wedding took place. So stay in the background, don't try to cut a dash in front of Eltham's neighbours; he'll think all the more of you if he sees that you know how to be discreet.'

All the family, including Mrs. Gainey, listened respectfully to Hester for she was a great source of worldly wisdom. Ada looked suitably grave. There was a testing time ahead of her, her whole future was in the melting-pot, and if she once left London there would be no one to run to for guidance.

At this moment the drawing-room door was opened with a flourish, and Mrs. Gainey's liveried manservant announced : 'The Marquess of Eltham.'

Every eye was turned on the slender, good-looking young man, with his fair hair fashionably ruffled, his pleasing air of unaffected friendliness and high spirits.

Jack, pausing on the threshold, was a little overwhelmed by the room which seemed so full of warmth and scent and furniture and young women in thin dresses with smooth, round arms, plump breasts and amber-red hair. A bevy of Golden Gaineys, all together, was inclined to be too luscious; he was grateful to his Ada for being different from the others, darker and slighter and in his view much more appealing.

She came forward to meet him, and he was glad to see her welcoming smile, for she had been annoyed and disconcerted when he suggested taking her into the country and he did not blame her.

Her sisters greeted him—he already knew them all— and the big, brassy mother whom he disliked because he thought Ada was afraid of her.

'I hope you mean to satisfy our curiosity, Lord Eltham,'

said Hester, gaily. 'Ada can talk of nothing but the house you are taking her to in Devonshire, but she seems to know very little about it, not even the name.'

'It is called Wilderness Cottage,' he replied, and immediately realised how little this would attract such a group of urban young women.

'Good God!' said Betsey. 'It sounds positively Gothic.'

Jack explained hastily that the wilderness was merely a strip of woodland running along the top of the cliffs at the boundary of his estate.

'The bushes and ferns grow down almost to the water's edge, and there is a very pretty footpath through the wood, with a fine view of the sea. It has always been a right of way, and indeed it is a famous haunt of travellers in search of the picturesque. The cottage itself is generally much admired.'

He was conscious as he spoke that this was not the sort of offer a man in his position was expected to make to a girl as sought-after as Ada, who might have insisted on a house in Mayfair, with first-rate lodgings at Brighton into the bargain. Unluckily he had spent too much of this year's allowance on hunting and other sports before he knew he was going to fall in love. He could not afford to hire a London house, now that his uncle had definitely refused to increase his allowance. And he had to provide a house of some sort, or Ada would send him packing and find a more generous protector. Of course he could go to the money-lenders, raise a loan on his expectations that was what nearly all his friends would have done. But Jack had an obsession about not getting into debt which was even stronger than his passion for Ada. It was founded (though he hardly realised this) on certain submerged memories of his very early childhood, of his father pleading and his mother crying, and a dreadful fear of some unknown disaster. . . . Much as he wanted Ada, he could not improve on Wilderness Cottage.

'I shall envy your rural solitude,' said Hester. 'You will have a charming summer. When do you set out?'

'As soon as Ada is ready.'

'Oh. Not quite immediately,' begged Ada. 'I must do some shopping. I haven't anything fit to wear in the country.'

The poor girl was too inexperienced to realise how little opportunity there would be for showing off new clothes in a place like Cleave. Still, she might as well buy herself a trousseau if it would give her pleasure; on this scale at least he was able to humour her.

Hester, catching his eye, said in a low voice: 'I perfectly understand your predicament.'

'You do?'

She moved her chair slightly, so that they were now facing each other in a tête-à-tête, and such was the force of her personality that her mother and sisters apparently took the hint and started talking among themselves in the room behind her.

'I was on fairly close terms with Lord Francis Aubrey,' she said, 'at the time of your father's death. I have never forgotten his exultation after the will was read.'

'Lord Francis rejoiced at my father's death? I cannot believe it.'

'I did not say that. He may have cared more for his brother than he does for most people. Who is to judge? I can only tell you that before your father was in his grave Lord Francis was speculating as to how things had been left. He has always liked the handling of money; I believe there are some rather strange stories—in short, he was extremely willing to take charge of all your possessions. You may say that this is no concern of mine, but I have Ada's future to consider. When a young woman leaves her friends and family and entrusts herself to a lover, she has a claim to be properly taken care of, sheltered from insult and inconvenience.'

'Yes, to be sure,' said Jack soberly. He had temporarily forgotten that Ada had left her friends and family twice before.

'I am certain you will do everything in your power to provide for her. It is a pity,' remarked Hester in the most casual manner, 'that you cannot find a satisfactory way of ending the Trust.'

'Hester!' said Sally from the window. 'A most unlucky circumstance. Lord Francis Aubrey has just turned the corner and I am pretty sure he is coming towards this house!'

Jack jumped like a guilty schoolboy. 'I don't want to meet him here!' He was aware that this sounded rather faint-hearted, and added: 'It doesn't do to have family disagreements in public. And besides, I'm afraid he might annoy Ada. He is so extremely outspoken.'

'Yes, you must both be out of the way.' Hester instantly took charge. They could hear someone knocking on the street door below. 'Ada, take Lord Eltham to the upper landing, and wait until Lord Francis is shown in here. Then you had better both go round to my house—no, he might come looking for you: Clarges Place would be safer. Can they go there, Betsey?'

'By all means. Ada may stay with me till they start for Devonshire, Corbet won't object.'

The loving couple were hustled away only just in time, for a moment later Lord Francis Aubrey walked in a yard ahead of the manservant who could not keep up with him.

Ignoring the three beautiful cyprians, he singled out their mother, marched straight up to her, and said: 'Good evening, ma'am. My name is Aubrey. I have something to say to your daughter Ada.'

Mrs. Gainey bridled. 'Ada is not at home, my lord. But I believe you are acquainted with my *eldest* daughter.'

Confronted with his former mistress, Lord Francis gave her an offhand nod. 'Pulling strings and making plans, as usual, Hester?'

'It's better than making enemies,' she replied sweetly.

Betsey laughed. Lord Francis looked her over as though she was a piece of cracked porcelain from an inferior dynasty, and asked with a note of disparagement, 'This one's not Ada, is she?'

He might be an insignificant little man, but he had inherited at least one talent from his ancestors, even if it was not a very agreeable one. He knew how to make lesser mortals feel uncomfortable. Betsey flushed and turned away.

'Ada is not here,' Hester assured him.

'A pity. You might warn her not to build too many hopes on my young nephew. No doubt he has promised her the moon—but unfortunately the moon is not in his gift. He is not able to set her up in the style for which she has been so carefully prepared . . .'

'Is that so? Poor Lord Eltham! His affairs must have been sadly mismanaged.'

Francis Aubrey's mouth hardened. 'I dare say he has not yet broken the news that he intends to carry your sister off into the depths of the country . . .'

'On the contrary, he has been extremely frank.'

'I am delighted to hear it. Even so, he will hardly have told you how dull she is going to be. Poor Eltham hasn't the least notion how to entertain a woman of pleasure.'

'I'll thank you not to miscall my daughter!' burst out Mrs. Gainey. 'The Marquess does not look on her in that light, and you will find yourself very awkwardly placed if he should happen to marry her.'

'Oh, Mother!' whispered Hester, exasperated. It was far too soon to start making capital out of this possibility.

'So that's the game, is it?' said Aubrey. 'Pray tell me, how much are you going to ask for my nephew's release?'

'If you think my sister could be bought off, once her affections were engaged . . .'

'I am perfectly certain that she could. I am equally certain that she won't be, if I have any say in the matter. We are not to be held to ransom by a conspiracy of harlots. I shall find some other means of getting rid of Miss Ada.'

## 4

The party from Lincoln's Inn arrived at Martland Farm in a hired carriage, having spent three days on the journey. This was about twice as long as a fast coach would have taken, but the children needed plenty of stops. They had been very crowded in the carriage; Nurse had little Emmie on her knee all the way, Laura was handed backwards and forwards between her mother and aunt, while Vinny and Ben, aged ten and seven, shared the fourth corner and got very cross. Lavinia's pug-dog Horace lay panting on the floor.

At last they left the turnpike road and bumped down a narrow lane towards the sea. The children began to get excited. Nurse said suspiciously, 'It's very quiet.' They were driving through a secluded combe; the hillside on their left was rampant with bracken, on their right the land had been half tamed and brought into cultivation. Lacy parasols of cow-parsley brushed the wheels of the carriage; moon daisies and ragged robin clustered in the grass.

They came to the farmhouse, a plain stone building with a slate roof and small, low windows. Mrs. Duffet, bustling and comfortable as ever, came out to meet them. She was delighted to see Lavinia and Caroline after so many years.

'And the children, ma'am—such little loves! We were ever so pleased to hear that you had such a fine family.'

Lavinia stood looking round her with an air of wonder. 'Look, Caro—the hayfield. And they've still got the dear old swing. And the clump of pinks outside the front door. Everything's just the same.'

She sounded quite happy about it, and Caroline was conscious of a feeling of relief.

Ben wanted a ride on the swing; Vinny asked: 'When can we go down to the sea?'

'Tomorrow,' said Lavinia. 'There will be plenty of to-morrows.'

The holiday had begun.

Mrs. Duffet escorted them indoors and up the steep, familiar stairs. Caroline had a little bedroom once allotted to Miss Mason, their governess, with a view across the valley of the wooded slopes above Martland Head, the place they called the Wilderness. She unpacked a few things, changed her dress thankfully after the hot journey, and went downstairs to the rather dark, dining-parlour which she found she remembered so well. The cloth was already laid.

'I've a nice bit of salmon for you,' said Mrs. Duffet, coming in after her. 'And a gooseberry pie. You were always partial to gooseberries in the old days, miss. It does me good to have you and Miss Lavinia back again, though I was very sorry to hear from Mrs. Harper about your poor Mama.'

Caroline made enquiries about the Duffet family and other old acquaintances.

'I believe Hoyle Park is unoccupied at present,' she added casually.

'Well, as to that, miss. I should not care to speak,' commented the farmer's wife with a prim expression. 'It's not the way I was brought up to think of the Family's being in residence—all the rooms under dust-sheets, and such irregular goings-on. But there, it's not my place to gossip about the Family.'

What could she mean? It was impossible to find out, as Lavinia was just coming downstairs. So Caroline spent the evening wondering who was at Hoyle Park, what they were doing, and whether there could be any repercussions that might upset Lavinia.

The next morning was so hot and fine that Lavinia decided they should start sea-bathing straight away. There was no telling how long the good weather would last. Cleave was not a resort like Weymouth or Brighton; there were no horse-drawn machines or muscular bathing-women, and anyone who tried to take a dip on the main beach would certainly collect an audience of rude fishermen, but Martland Mouth was so extremely private—a mere nick in the cliffs at the end of a solitary combe—you could safely undress in a cave and walk boldly across the strip of beach with only the gulls to look on. This was how Mrs. Prior and her daughters had bathed in the old days; Vinny and Ben Reed had been brought up on Mama's stories about dipping in the sea at Martland, and they ran happily down the farm-track ahead of their mother and aunt, for a first sight of the English Channel glittering blue-green at the sudden end of the land.

By the time they had undressed in the company of a dead starfish and put on the odd, enveloping flannel pantaloons and chemises that had been specially made for them in London, Ben's courage began to falter. Shivering a little as he came out of the cave, he said: 'The water must be very deep? Are you sure we can stand up in it?'

'It's not deep at the edges, silly,' scoffed his sister. 'Did you think it was the same all the way across to France?'

'Now, Vinny—don't be unkind to your little brother,' said Lavinia. 'Pay no attention to her, my love. Mama will take care of you.'

Ben, seizing his advantage, said that Vinny was a nasty, horrid girl and (inconsequently) that he wasn't going into the sea after all.

Vinny looked contemptuous, Lavinia distracted, and Caroline, who was used to scenes of this sort, firmly seized each child by an arm and said: 'Come along! Let's see who's the first to get their feet wet!'

Getting wet feet was generally a forbidden delight; Ben forgot to be frightened as they stepped over the pebbles and ran across the crisp sand. Soon the water was over their ankles, their knees, they were wading up to their waists, and the children were squeaking from all sorts of sensations, cold, surprise, excitement, but not fear. It was difficult to persuade Ben to dip down and let the sea lap right over his shoulders, but he managed it in the end, and was really sorry when it was time to come out.

There was a hot breakfast waiting for them at the farm, after which the intrepid bathers rested for a couple of hours to recover from their exertions.

About eleven Lavinia and Caroline decided to walk into the village and call on their mother's old friend Mrs. Harper.

'We ought to go the very first day,' said Lavinia. 'We owe her that attention.'

And we shall be able to find out what is happening at Hoyle Park, thought Caroline, and which of the Aubreys are scandalising Mrs. Duffet.

The large country parish of Cleave was contained by two adjacent combes, each running down to its own tiny bay. Cleave itself was the one where the village was situated; the only buildings in Martland were those connected with the farm. All the land in the parish belonged to Lord Eltham, but the headland between the two valleys was actually inside the Hoyle Park enclosure. The house stood back about a mile from the sea, surrounded by gardens and grassland; the property was shut in on three sides by a high wall, but the southern boundary provided its own natural barrier: a stretch of wooded cliffs, diving inaccessibly towards the sea. So Hoyle Park stood like an impregnable fortress between Cleave and Martland, and if you wanted to go by carriage from one to the other, you were obliged to drive up the lane on to the turnpike road, and down the next lane into the valley beyond. If you were on foot, however, you could take a right of way across the headland which was known as the Wilderness Walk.

The two sisters climbed the steep path which straggled up the hillside. It was hot and windless, and they were glad to reach the estate wall with its narrow wicket-gate leading into the wood.

Suddenly they were in a different world: a place of soft green depths, of golden green leaf patterns and transparencies. There was a curiously hushed atmosphere in the wood, yet within this shell of silence there were many small individual sounds—the shiver of branches, the stealthy padding of hidden animals, the droning of insects, the hopping and fluttering and thin, high songs of birds in the trees overhead.

The Wilderness Walk was a moss-grown footpath, about three feet wide, that wandered through the wood in a series of graceful loops, vaguely following the line of the coast. On their left Lavinia and Caroline could see an occasional sweep of open turf; on their right the ground began to fall away, so that the bushes and trees of the Wilderness seemed to be rushing headlong towards the cliff's edge and over, into the opaque blue sea, as it shimmered out there in the morning heat.

They strolled at a leisurely pace, enjoying the beauty of the scenery, while Horace the Pug pounded along on his short legs in a state of ecstasy. He had never dreamed of such an Elysium, poor London-bred animal.

Presently they came to a clearing on the landward side of the path. There was a pretty little house built of the local stone, with a patch of front garden full of stocks and pansies, neatly squared off by a clipped hedge.

'I wonder who's living there now,' remarked Caroline. 'Some retired chaplain or tutor, I dare say.'

Wilderness Cottage had been designed as a refuge sixty years ago by the eccentric third Marquess who thought he was being persecuted by the Pope. His successors had used it to house various protégés of the family, and when she was a little girl Caroline had always thought it would be a wonderful place to live. She looked around with interest for signs of the present tenant—there certainly was a tenant, for there were curtains in all the windows, and the front door was standing ajar—but there was not a soul in sight.

The path across the headland was rather over a mile long, and for the last hundred yards it joined the end of the carriage drive, both finishing up at the massive gates which formed a suitably imposing entrance to Hoyle Park. There was of course a lodge with a lodge-keeper in attendance, but he was not expected to throw wide the huge iron portals for the benefit of mere foot-passengers; there was a humble door in the wall which they could open for themselves.

Caroline and Lavinia went through this door, straight from the sylvan solitude of the Wilderness into the busy village of Cleave. The grey streets descended like a flight of stairs to the tiny harbour. There were boats bobbing about in the water and nets drying on the shingle, and most of the activity was concentrated down there. The upper part of the village was more genteel. It was dominated by an ancient church; just below the church stood a prosperous inn, and below that again, immediately opposite the Hoyle Park gates, was an elegant row of modern villas known as Belvedere Terrace.

The first house in the row belonged to Mrs. Harper, and as they crossed the road they could see her sitting in her window, gazing out. She saw them coming, and began to wave.

A moment later they were being ushered into her tiny drawing-room.

'Come in, come in,' said the old lady, turning slightly in her chair. 'You will forgive my not rising to greet you, I'm afraid such civilities are beyond me now . . . Let me look at you both. Lavinia's still a beauty, I see. And Caroline—why aren't you married?'

'Because nobody's asked me, ma'am,' said Caroline, laughing. It was no good taking umbrage at any frank speaking from Mrs. Harper.

'Stuff!' said her hostess. 'The young men must be fools. Well, God knows, most of them are.'

Caroline was shocked by her appearance. When she was a child this elderly friend of her mother's had seemed at least a hundred years old, but an energetic and commanding figure as she stumped about the village. Now, at the actual age of seventy-five, she was dreadfully frail, a prisoner in a chair, her swollen, arthritic hands lying in her lap, for she was no longer able to sew. She read a great deal, she told them, and was lucky in having so many visitors.

'I sit here and watch the world go by, and what I can't make out for myself is generally related to me by one of my faithful band of spies. Which reminds me, did you happen to see Eltham's bird of paradise, as you came through the Wilderness?'

'A bird?' repeated Lavinia. 'I don't think—is it flying about in the wood?'

'Sitting on her nest, so I'm told. My dear child, I am speaking of his mistress. He has brought her down from London; she is one of a family of notorious courtesans, what they call a Fashionable Impure—you can imagine how our tongues are wagging.'

Lavinia looked grave, and Mrs. Harper asked her rather tartly whether she'd turned Methody?

Lavinia was suffering not only from moral scruples, but also from a chronic anxiety whenever the Aubrey family was mentioned, caused by her dread of meeting Lord Francis.

Caroline decided to come to her rescue, which she did

by saying: 'Excuse me, ma'am; can you tell me who is that gingerbread dandy down there in the street? I never saw anyone like him in Cleave before.'

He was a young man of about twenty-one wearing an absurdly high neckcloth, a rather loud cinnamon-coloured coat with too many brass buttons, and a pair of yellow nankeen pantaloons so tight that she wondered whether he could sit down in them. He kept taking off his hat to salute every female who passed, exhibiting a cascade of Byronic dark locks which must have taken him a long time to dissarrange. His face, however, was not Byronic; it was the plump cherub-face of a mischievous little boy.

'Oh, that's Tavy Barrow,' said Mrs. Harper. 'From the Rectory, you know. Isn't he a figure of fun?'

'Tavy?' said Lavinia. 'Do you mean the little one, the youngest of that great family?'

'Yes, Octavius. I am sorry for him, poor fellow, with such venerable parents, and those seven elder brothers all doing so well in the Navy or the Church, I fancy he feels obliged to strike out a new line for himself. He is up at Oxford—that is to say, he has been sent down for the rest of the term, he won't say why, but he is in disgrace with his father. He is supposed to be engaged in making a new catalogue of the library up at the Park. Not that they need one, I imagine, but it was good-natured of Eltham to give him something to do.'

Octavius Barrow looked towards the window at that moment. Mrs. Harper raised her hand imperiously; he came instantly across to Belvedere Terrace and was admitted to the house.

Seen at close quarters, the cherub-face had a pair of eyes that were as bright and black as currants, full of a kind of innocent malice.

He was introduced to Lavinia and Caroline, insisted that he remembered them perfectly, and sat down with a certain amount of caution.

'What news from the Park, Tavy?' demanded Mrs. Harper.

'Eltham was in a great taking yesterday, ma'am, when he received a letter from his mother. He thought she might be coming south. But I am happy to tell you that her ladyship is fixed in Scotland for the time being. Lady Lucy, you know. Always so unpunctual. None of Eltham's family is here on the spot, lucky devil,' said Octavius with feeling, 'but he is almost afraid to open his letters in case Lord Francis has written round to inform them all that he has installed the beauteous Ada in the Wilderness. Which is just the sort of shabby thing that Lord Francis would do.'

'I dare say,' said Mrs. Harper. She looked thoughtfully at Lavinia, and changed the subject.

Presently Lavinia signed to Caroline, and they rose to leave. Octavius remained behind, to tell Mrs. Harper some more of the gossip that he seemed to collect instinctively, like a bee collecting honey.

'I know she is a sick woman,' remarked Lavinia, as they walked back through the Wilderness. 'One should not grudge her any pleasure that is within her reach. And I have noticed that people who grew up in the last century are not always as refined as we would wish today. Even so, Mrs. Harper should not have encouraged that very odd young man to run on as he did. Not while you were there, at any rate. Unmarried girls are supposed to remain ignorant of such things.'

'A woman who did not know that men have mistresses would be extremely ill-prepared for marriage,' said Caroline. 'Besides, now I come to think of it, I've already seen

Lord Eltham's inamorata, and I must say she is ravishingly pretty.'

'What do you mean? How can you have seen her?'

'Don't you remember the day I called in Berkeley Square, I told you that Eltham arrived just as I was leaving? I was sure at the time that it was him, and I suppose his companion was the same young woman.'

'It might not have been. He sounds very dissolute.'

'Well, he looks charming,' said Caroline with a touch of defiance.

They were again passing Wilderness Cottage; she glanced hopefully over the hedge, but there was still no one to be seen.

## 5

'I wish you would go out more often,' said Jack, gazing in perplexity at what he could see of Ada's white discontented face as she turned it obstinately away from him. 'Take a walk in the wood. Or down by the sea. Or we could go for a drive.'

Ada didn't want to go for a drive. 'And I hate your old wood, it's nothing but dirt and flies and brambles.'

Jack was hurt by this description of his beloved Wilderness, but he was convinced that Ada was very unhappy, though he could not fathom why. Perhaps the solitude affected her in a way that a countryman could not appreciate. The tall trees that surrounded the clearing did give the place a feeling of melancholy. There was not much light in the cottage, and the furniture was old and plain.

He had tried to improve the rooms by bringing over a few trifles from his own house—screens and ornaments and even pictures. And he had remembered, before they left London, to order a dozen of the latest novels and several albums of music for Ada's entertainment. He was rather proud of this act of devotion and reminded her of it now.

'What's the good of having music when there isn't an instrument to play on?'

'You are very welcome to come and use the pianoforte at the Park.'

Ada promptly burst into tears.

Jack felt that he was being badly treated. If he had persuaded any respectable young woman to become his mistress, he might have expected—and deserved—some violent demonstrations of anguish. It was supposed to be an advantage of dealing with girls like the Golden Gaineys that they knew all the rules beforehand and never made trouble. So what was wrong with Ada?

(It did not occur to him that Hester Gainey would have been just as disconcerted as he was by the behaviour of her youngest sister. But Ada had escaped from Hester's jurisdiction and she had her own ideas about the best way of getting what she wanted.)

'What have I said now to distress you?' he asked in some exasperation. 'I simply suggested you should come up to the house.'

'Yes, to creep in and play the pianoforte by myself, so long as there is no one there to be contaminated!'

'My dearest girl, you are being perfectly absurd . . .'

'Oh, am I? Are you going to invite all the county to meet me?'

Jack was silenced.

'I dare say some of the gentlemen will be glad to ogle

your mistress,' she added bitterly. 'They will get very drunk and expect me to dance on the table.'

Jack took her in his arms and began trying to kiss some sense into her. Ada immediately shut her mouth and her eyes and slumped into inertia. She had been playing this trick on him ever since they arrived in Devonshire, and it was driving him demented. He wanted her so badly that he felt almost ill with desire, yet he was too gentle to use force against such a beautiful, defenceless creature.

'Ada, for God's sake tell me why you are unhappy? Is it my fault? What have I got to do to be forgiven?'

Ada said that he ought to know very well what was the matter: she was lonely, she was frightened, everyone here despised her—she had not understood, she said, living among her sisters and their set in London, how the world regarded girls like them—but now she had no one belonging to her and no money . . .

'My darling, you must not give way to such fancies,' exclaimed Jack, his generous heart full of pity. 'I'll always take care of you, as long as you live. I promise.'

'You haven't any money either,' she pointed out. 'Not until you marry.'

'Well then, we'll be married,' he said recklessly. He could not bear to see her so wretched, and he was by now ready to pay almost any price for the privilege of being allowed to make love to her.

This did stop her crying, though she still was not satisfied.

'Do you mean a hole-and-corner wedding that you can repudiate later on?'

'Certainly not! I have given you no reason to think so ill of me.'

'Then will you present me to your family as your future

wife? I must be properly acknowledged by them before I can agree.'

Jack thought of his family, of his mother so fastidious that the most high-minded young lady would hardly be good enough for her only son; of his uncle—but he then decided it would be wiser not to think about Lord Francis in this connection; his married sisters and their husbands ought to be more tolerant than the older generation, only he didn't feel very hopeful about ambitious Maria and her Member of Parliament, or serious Lucy and her Scottish laird. Of course there was Anne.

She was the youngest of the family, not yet twenty-one, and she had been a handful even in the schoolroom. Wayward, a flirt, by the time she came out she could only be described as fast. Her marriage to Philip Dangerfield, a young man with no money, had been sanctioned simply to stop them running away together. Surely he could count on Anne's having some sympathy for Ada? And the Dangerfields were living less than fifty miles away in Somerset.

'You know that most of my family are too far off to be consulted,' he said. 'However my youngest sister and her husband are within reach. I shall drive over to Alcheston tomorrow, stay the night, and get them to come back with me on Tuesday. How will that serve? You will like Anne extremely, and once you have met her your position will be much more established.'

'But will she agree to come?'

'She will if I ask her to,' he said, rather grandly.

Ada looked at him for a moment; then she threw her arms round him and buried her face against his shoulder. 'Oh, Jack, my dear Jack, what a brute I am! I never believed that you would be so noble and good. I don't deserve so much kindness.'

Jack was so gratified by this spontaneous affection that it distracted him from the slight awkwardness of not being certain whether they were engaged.

In any case the uncertainty saved him from having to consider too closely what it would be like marrying into the Gainey family and having that old harridan for a mother-in-law.

He intended to make an early start on Monday, but was delayed by one thing and another (including a long and tender parting from Ada) and it was nearly midday when he finally set off down the avenue in his Stanhope gig, followed by a groom on horseback, for there was no room for a passenger in the little chairlike conveyance. He was still some way from the lodge gates when they were unexpectedly opened by the lodge-keeper to let another carriage come in from the road.

It was a curricle and pair driven by Lord Francis Aubrey. The very last person he wanted to see.

However, there was no avoiding him. The curricle approached, the two horses sweating from a long, hilly run, and Lord Francis perched up on his high-sprung seat above the wheels. Just like a monkey on a stick, thought his nephew disrespectfully. He had a liveried groom sitting behind him.

The carriages drew level, each driver resentfully hugging his own verge, and both reined in.

'What are you doing here?' demanded Jack.

'I've come to inspect our ancestral acres.'

'Oh. Well, I cannot turn back now. I'm just off to Alcheston.'

'Indeed? And what have you done with the fascinating Ada? Have you fallen out with her already? I could have warned you what would happen. Females of that profession are not at all good company once you take them out of their own setting. They are like certain types of claret, they don't travel.'

Jack frowned. 'I should like a word with you in private, if you please.'

'We are fairly private already, as far as I can see,' said his uncle, gazing about him at the grass and trees, and completely ignoring the two grooms. He always said exactly what he liked in front of the servants, a habit Jack had never been able to imitate.

Seeing his agonised expression, Lord Francis said in a pitying way, 'I don't suppose anything you have to tell me is likely to surprise Tunstall. Or Roberts either. Good morning, Roberts,' he added, as an afterthought to Jack's groom.

'Good morning, my lord,' said Roberts, looking down his nose and trying not to laugh.

Jack knew he was being deliberately provoked. The little man was like a gadfly at times. He got out of the gig. 'If you please, sir,' he repeated stiffly.

After a moment Lord Francis followed him.

When they had walked a short distance from the carriages, Jack brought out his news with no attempt at finesse. 'I must tell you that I have asked Ada to marry me.'

He watched his uncle's face. All the mockery had gone out like light . . . Francis Aubrey was suddenly angry.

'Good God, you ought not to be allowed out without a keeper! Is she pregnant?'

'No. At least—I don't think so.' (Could this be the explanation of Ada's fits of nervous depression?)

'You don't think so! You have not even considered the most serious consequences of putting that little strumpet in the place that once belonged to your mother. And mine.

45

Haven't you any sense of what is fitting? At present you think you are in love—well, there's nothing uncommon in that, and you are already taking the best cure. The girl's got nothing to sell that you haven't bought and paid for; what the devil do you hope to gain by marrying her?'

The answer to this was, of course, that the mere fact of his marriage—to anyone at all—would put an end to the hated Trust, but Jack's emotions had been so worked on by feelings of compassion (towards Ada) and indignation (towards Francis) that he had honestly forgotten this prosaic motive, so he was able to say in a very lofty manner that it was repugnant to him to think of choosing a wife as if he was buying a heifer, though naturally he would not expect Uncle Francis to understand this. He wanted to rescue Ada from her unhappy situation; he said a good deal about her earnest desire to lead a different sort of life, and the delicacy of mind that had survived in most unlikely surroundings. 'And to prove that,' he concluded, 'I can tell you, sir, that instead of jumping at my offer and wanting to be married without delay, she has refused to give me an answer, refused even to come up to the house, until she is made welcome there by a member of my family. Even you must admit that she is behaving very well, and it does her great credit.'

Lord Francis admitted nothing. He merely said, 'Is that why you are going to see Anne?'

'Yes. That is to say—I had intended to bring her back with me tomorrow. . . .'

He had just realised that if he went off and left Ada unprotected Francis would be able to go down to the cottage, to coerce and threaten her into giving up any hope of marriage. He had no legal right to interfere but Ada might not understand this. Francis was so clever in his devious way, and he had a cruel tongue. Poor little Ada would be no match for him.

Francis must have guessed what Jack was thinking, for he said, in a more moderate voice, 'You had better go to Alcheston and talk to Anne. I am sure her opinions will be more acceptable than mine. You need not hesitate to leave Ada; I'll guarantee not to go near the cottage until you return.'

Jack was surprised by this unexpected offer of a truce. He did very much want to go and see his sister; he needed her support and he did not think he would get it unless he could explain the whole situation to her in person. An appeal in writing would not have the same effect; he was not very good at expressing himself in a letter. So he took his uncle's unusual fit of chivalry at its face value, and decided to stick to his plan and go to Alcheston after all.

He got back into the gig and drove away. Francis Aubrey continued to stand in the avenue for several minutes, apparently sunk in meditation.

## 6

A little after two o'clock on Tuesday Caroline was sitting in a small stone gazebo at the very end of the Hoyle Park wall, overlooking Martland combe and the sea. Vinny and Ben were playing in the gorse and bracken on the hillside, and Horace the pug was sniffing around for rabbits.

It was their sixth day in Devonshire. They had bathed, as usual, for the weather was still very fine, and then spent most of the morning on the beach collecting shells, which were to be polished, carefully graded according to size and shape, and eventually used to decorate boxes and pin-trays in a very artistic manner. Lavinia had given herself a headache from so much stooping in the hot sun; she was lying down; Nurse and the younger children were in the garden at the back of the farmhouse, but Vinny and Ben, after a light luncheon and a compulsory rest, had begged to go out again and play in the combe. So Caroline had volunteered to keep an eye on them.

'But don't imagine you can wheedle me into running about any more today,' she told them. 'I shall sit in the watch tower and keep cool.'

She had named it the watch tower when she was Vinny's age; the odd, unnecessary little hut had always intrigued her. The high enclosure wall of Hoyle Park came to a sudden end at the place where the ground began to splinter and split away, high up on the cliff-face at the corner of Martland Mouth. Beyond this point no wall was required, for although the woody headland jutted some way further over the sea, it was quite impossible to climb up into the Wilderness from the rocks below. The wall ran on for about twenty feet beyond the wicket-gate and then stopped. Perhaps the builder thought it might look rather ridiculous if his fine wall broke off sharp, he had punctuated his design by adding a glorified sentry-box to act as a full stop. There was a rustic bench inside, and Caroline had an excellent panorama of the cliffs dropping away on her left, the hillside with the children playing in the foreground, and the valley opening towards the sea. The tide was out, and the wet sand shone like a mirror. If she looked inland she could see the lane, the roof of the farmhouse, and the blobs of trees in the orchard. And much closer at hand, the wicket-gate and the estate wall running along the crest of the hill.

It was all very peaceful; there was only one small cloud

to threaten her contentment. She had overheard the farm people saying that Lord Francis Aubrey had arrived at the Park, unexpectedly, the day before. It was extremely annoying, and she hoped Lavinia would not find out that the man who had once jilted her was here in the same village, as she would probably work herself into a fit of nervous palpitations. Perhaps a hint to Mrs. Duffet would be in order? The chances of their actually meeting Lord Francis were fairly remote.

Ben and Vinny were making a house in the bracken. Every now and then they would run into the wood and come back with some treasure in the way of ferns or foxgloves. She had been sitting there about ten minutes when she noticed that one of the party was missing.

'Where's Horace?' she called out.

Vinny gazed about her vaguely, and Ben said: 'He went into the wood.'

'Did he? I suppose he can come to no harm.' All the same Caroline knew that one ought not to let an animal run wild on someone else's property; after a struggle with the pleasures of inertia, she got up and went in search of Horace, taking the children with her.

They passed through the squeaky gate; the wood was dark after the open brightness of the combe, and filled with a greenish, under-water light, though still very hot. The wind that always blew on the headland fanned the tops of the tallest trees; it could not penetrate the layers of torpid branches or the dense maze of bushes and briars.

Caroline and the children walked along the mossy path, calling: 'Horace! Horace!'

There was no sign of the little dog.

Caroline had a curious feeling of time being suspended. There was something mysterious about the Wilderness, and

the cottage in the heart of the Wilderness, where Lord
Eltham's mistress lived like a dispossessed princess in a
fairy-tale. A phrase flashed through Caroline's mind: *La
Belle Au Bois Dormant*. Not the sleeping beauty, as in
English, but more romantically, its French equivalent, the
beauty in the sleeping wood.

They had reached the cottage, and for the first time,
they caught a glimpse of Ada Gainey. A chair had been
brought out into the garden, and a young woman in a light
muslin dress was sitting there alone, a few feet away from
them. Caroline recognised the dark-eyed siren she had met
outside Eltham House a fortnight ago.

She came to a halt, and for a long moment the two girls
stared at each other. Caroline would have liked to speak,
yet she felt somehow silenced by the cyprian's answering
gaze of cool defiance. As she stood there, stupidly uncertain of herself, Vinny broke the spell.

'There he is—there's Horace!'

And there he was, a plump and panting little hunter with
a swashbuckling look in his eye. He came trotting up to
them, to be scolded and caressed, and they turned back
towards Martland.

The girl in the white dress was still sitting in the garden.
From the cottage window behind her came the high sweet
note of a clock chiming the half-hour.


## 7


The lime avenue at Hoyle Park ran straight up to the house
without any fanciful turns or detours. The house itself was
a grey Tudor building, well suited to the condition of the

Aubreys who had first lived there as untitled country gentlemen. Jack's grandfather had refaced the south front in a more modern style, and added an orangery, but that was all, and Jack had often felt that he preferred this dignified and moderate dwelling-house to his Palladian mansion in Kent.

But as he drove up the avenue in the torpid heat of Tuesday afternoon, he was in no mood to admire fine groves of trees, or carved stonework and oriel windows. He could think of nothing but what he was going to say to Lord Francis.

For that devious little man, when encouraging him to go and visit Anne, had failed to mention that he himself had spent the previous night at Alcheston, on his way down from London, and that he had already given the Dangerfields a most unfavourable description of Ada. Jack had reached his sister's house, hungry for sympathy, only to find Anne up in arms at the thought of such a horrid creature desecrating her beloved Wilderness, while Philip insisted on giving him a lot of worldly advice. It was altogether intolerable.

He stamped into his own hall in a perfect fever of righteous rage, to be told by the butler that Lord Francis had left the house about an hour ago, without saying where he was going. So there was no excuse for putting off the coming scene with Ada. There would be a scene he thought gloomily, when she heard that his mission had failed. He changed his clothes, fortified himself with a plate of cold chicken and a glass of wine, and set off across the park.

He reached Wilderness Cottage at three o'clock.

There was a dining-room chair placed on the tiny patch of grass just inside the hedge: nothing else unusual and no one in sight. The door of the cottage stood ajar. He went in, exclaiming: 'Butterfly—I'm back,' on a note of jubilation. (No sense in upsetting the poor girl before he had to.)

The parlour was empty, his ridiculous love-name hung in the unresponsive air, mocking him.

He heard the sound of a footstep in the room overhead, and ran up the steep flight of stairs, to be met at the top by Molly Thatcher, a stout young woman who had been sent to look after the cottage, helped out in shifts by various other servants from the park.

'Oh, my lord—you did give me a start, to be sure.' She was not a very polished domestic.

'Where's Miss Ada, Molly?'

'I don't rightly know, my lord. I went up to the gardens for to see whether Mr. Budden had any ripe strawberries, Miss having said as how she'd fancy some. She was out by the rose-bush when I left her, and the dear knows where she is now, for I haven't seen her since. She's clean vanished. 'Tis very strange.'

'I expect she's gone for a walk.'

'Without a bonnet or a retty-cool? And in those little kid slippers? Besides which, she don't never go out a-walking, my lord,' insisted Molly, who was determined to make some dramatic capital out of Ada's absence.

Jack took himself into the parlour to wait, Ada wouldn't stay out long in this heat. He forced himself to contain his growing impatience until half-past three, when he went into the kitchen and asked Molly what time she had left Ada alone at the cottage. Molly did not know, but it was clear that she hadn't hurried over the strawberry picking, and he remembered that she was keeping company with one of his under-gardeners. Working backwards, he thought that Ada might have been out for about an hour.

He decided to go and look for her.

Once outside the cottage he turned right-handed towards Martland. He did not think Ada would have gone to the village she was almost too keenly aware of her own invidious position, and wouldn't deliberately flaunt herself alone in a public place. He soon reached the wicket-gate. The hinges squeaked, as they always did, and he saw a movement in the little stone gazebo at the end of the wall, a flash of some light, feminine material, lilac and white stripes.

'So there you are, my dear. I was wondering where . . . Oh! I beg your pardon.' He found himself confronting a young woman several years older than Ada, and pretty rather than beautiful, with a brown complexion and a lively, sensitive face. He said abruptly, 'I mistook you for someone else.'

There was no proper answer to this statement.

She said gravely and without coquetry, 'I am sorry you were disappointed.'

'I wonder whether perhaps you have seen the person I am looking for? She must have gone down into the combe. Have you been sitting here long?'

'The best part of an hour, and no one has passed through the gate in either direction during that time.' She hesitated. 'Is it—are you speaking of the young lady who is living in the cottage? She was there in the garden at half-past two, and she certainly hasn't come into the combe since then.'

'Oh, she was still there at half-past two? Did you happen to notice anything particular—what she was doing— but, why should you, after all?'

'Well, I don't know that she was doing anything except

sit in a chair. I only saw her for a moment; I had gone into the wood with my nephew and niece to fetch our little dog.'

Jack became vaguely aware of two children and a puppy, rolling in the bracken some distance away.

'I can't think where she's gone,' he said, half to himself. Adding, ingenuously, 'It's very odd, for she hates walking. She's not at all partial to country life.'

'How provoking for you,' said the girl in the lilac stripes.

She then blushed furiously, and Jack woke up to the fact that she knew who he was, who—or rather what— Ada was, and realised that she ought to have preserved an air of young-lady-like incomprehension.

He looked at her again, he had an idea he had seen her somewhere recently. 'Have we not met before?'

'Not for twelve years, Lord Eltham. The last time, I remember, you tried to put a frog down my neck.'

He was so dumbfounded by this that she took pity on him.

'I am Caroline Prior; I dare say you will have forgotten my existence. When I was a child we used to come to Martland every summer.'

A series of images spiralled up to the surface of his mind, of the year when they had been thrown into each other's unwilling society because it suited their families.

'You got my favourite kite stuck in a tree, and re-arranged my collection of fossils. I certainly haven't forgotten you, Miss Prior. How could I?'

'Oh dear, was I very interfering? I'm afraid it is my besetting sin. I dare say I deserved the frog.'

They studied each other with a rueful amusement. Jack said, 'I suppose you are staying at the farm?'

The children came up while they were talking, and Caroline asked them whether they remembered seeing a lady in the cottage garden. Yes, they had seen her, but they both agreed with their aunt she had not come out of the wood.

He thanked them all for their assistance, and retreated into the Wilderness.

As he closed the gate, he heard the small boy ask: 'Why did that man want to find the pretty lady, Aunt Caro?'

And Caroline Prior's brisk reply. 'I have not the least idea, my love, and it is no business of ours.'

He felt he had made rather a fool of himself in front of that sharp-witted girl, and for no good reason, because of course Ada would be back at the cottage by now.

Ada was not at the cottage. Molly was waiting on the doorstep to tell him so.

'I reckon she's lost herself in the Wilderness, my lord.'

Jack thought this very unlikely, for he could not imagine Ada wandering far enough to get lost. The Wilderness was an absolute maze of clambering bushes and saplings, but though there were a number of narrow tracks used by children and rustics, they would not be at all enticing to a pampered London girl in a muslin dress and thin shoes. The only path that Ada would recognise as such was the Wilderness Walk itself, and she could hardly have got lost on that well-trodden thoroughfare. Extraordinary as it might seem, she must have gone to the village.

He was already halfway there before he had settled this idea in his mind: walking fast and glancing to left and right, just in case she had strayed off course, but there was no sign of her. He came to the carriage drive, the great gateway, and the door in the wall beside it. He was just about to summon the lodge-keeper, when he looked across the village street at the row of elegant modern houses and caught sight of old Mrs. Harper. She sat in her window all day and was reputed to notice everything that went on. Here was someone who would be able to tell him whether or not Ada had really ventured into Cleave.

He presented himself at the front door of Number One, Belvedere Terrace and asked if Mrs. Harper would receive him, without considering exactly how he was going to frame his questions to that astute old busybody.

He was shown into her drawing-room and made exceedingly welcome.

'Why, my dear Eltham,' exclaimed Mrs. Harper, turning stiffly in her chair. 'This is handsome of you. I am sure you have better things to do than calling on ancient cripples.'

Jack felt guilty. He was a very kind young man and did not want her to guess that he had come simply in search of information. So he sat down and made conversation, oppressed by the number of objects in that small space: Chelsea cupids and Venetian dolphins, miniatures and cameos in little frames, glass paperweights, lockets and trinkets of Battersea enamel, a mouse carved out of a peachstone which he had greatly admired as a child . . . He always felt twice his normal size in Mrs. Harper's house, and he knew he must appear to her as a sadly plebeian figure, with his plain coat and pantaloons, and his cropped hair.

'What an excellent view you have from this window,' he remarked at last. 'I am sure you see everything that goes on.'

'I would gladly exchange my window for a serviceable pair of legs,' she said drily.

Jack was abashed.

'But I should not complain. I own I do get a great deal of diversion from the prospect before me.'

'I am told that you can always give a complete list of everyone who comes into the village from the Wilderness. Is that possible? This afternoon, for instance: did you notice any new faces?'

Mrs. Harper shot him a speculating glance but answered quite seriously.

'Well, there was very little coming and going. Jem Heard took the short-cut some time after midday, and returned about two hours later—I suppose he had been over to do some work for Mr. Duffet at the farm. However, you can hardly rank Jem as a stranger.' He was in fact the son of the estate carpenter. 'There was quite a crowd came out of the wood at a quarter past one; townsfolk in their Sunday best, I judged them to be a wedding-party out for a jollification. They spent some time at the Ship, and were driven away in an old waggon, dressed over all with ribbons and favours Then there was a young couple in the early afternoon; quite respectable people. They went off in a gig that was waiting for them in the road. That was the sum total. Naturally I saw you returning from Alcheston.'

'Are you sure there was no one else?'

'Whom were you expecting?' enquired Mrs. Harper.

Jack did not answer. A painful suspicion was forming in his mind. 'This couple. What were they like?'

'Oh, he was a big, strong fellow with a fine pair of shoulders. I couldn't tell you much about his companion, she was wearing a very silly bonnet. Now that females display so much of their figures I dare say they feel obliged to hide their faces.'

According to Molly, Ada had not been wearing a bonnet, silly or otherwise, but Jack had forgotten this for the

57

moment, being plunged into a state of doubt and jealousy. For if she had not come out of the Wilderness alone, surely she must be the anonymous woman whom the stranger had taken off in a gig? Jack had told her not to expect him back from Alcheston until this evening; wasn't it all too likely that she might have gone for a drive with another man? A former lover perhaps, who had pursued her down to Devonshire? He could not help remembering the way she had lived until now, the corrupting influence of her mother and sisters.

He escaped from Mrs. Harper as quickly as he could, determined to call at the Ship Inn on the chance that Ada's hypothetical admirer might be staying there.

The Ship was just above Belvedere Terrace, a few yards further up the hill. It was a well-appointed place and did a good trade. Visitors who wanted to follow the famous Wilderness Walk along the coast were in the habit of sending their carriages round by road to meet them at the Ship.

Sam Roebuck, the landlord, was only too ready to oblige the Marquess. What might he have the honour of doing for his lordship?

Jack mentioned the couple described by Mrs. Harper. Had Roebuck seen them? Was the gentleman possibly staying at the Inn? The question was tentative; he was surprised by the vehemence of the answer.

'No, my lord! That person—for gentleman I will not call him—has not set foot in this house. I do not know his name but I can tell you his calling. He is a London wine-merchant,' said Mr. Roebuck with loathing.

'Indeed?' said Jack, rather taken aback by this animosity.

'He has been visiting Plymouth on business, I understand, accompanied by his wife, who was wishful to walk through the Wilderness, my lord, being interested in plants and such. So they left their carriage at the top of Martland combe and sent it on here to wait for them. The groom—an impudent Cockney—came in to wet his whistle, and Joe asked him if his master had given any orders for refreshment, and if the lady would care to take tea, which our female visitors very often do. And the little upstart had the insolence to boast that his master was a wine merchant in a very superior situation—in Duke Street, St. James's, I believe—and that he would not demean himself by drinking at a village alehouse. I was never so angry in my life, considering the eight years I spent in the service of your lordship's father, and all the distinguished patrons I've had the privilege of entertaining at the Ship, am I to be weighed in the balance and found wanting by a common tradesman?'

Jack murmured a few words of consolation. He had lost interest in the stranger as soon as he heard of the business in Plymouth and the botanising wife. Besides which, a new thought had struck him. Surely all the people listed by Mrs. Harper must have passed the cottage before half-past two, or Caroline Prior would have seen them, either in the wood itself, or at the wicket-gate during the time she was in the gazebo? But Caroline had seen no one except Ada, alone in the cottage garden. His dear little Ada, he was ashamed of having doubted her. Relief and remorse were both swept aside by a new anxiety, for if Ada had not come out at either end of the Wilderness Walk, then she was still somewhere in the grounds of Hoyle Park, and what could possibly have happened to her?

'And how was Alcheston?' asked Francis Aubrey. 'How was Anne? I trust you enjoyed your visit?'

He was standing at the bottom of the oak staircase, having put on a black coat and white waistcoat in which to eat his dinner.

Jack had just come in, after one more fruitless visit to the cottage; he had spent some time aimlessly casting about and calling Ada's name before finally admitting that there was a real cause for alarm. He had then run the whole way across the park, and was too anxious and preoccupied to remember that he had a bone to pick with Francis.

He blurted out his news. 'Ada's disappeared.'

There was a short pause.

'I'm sorry, my dear boy,' said Lord Francis. 'But these girls are seldom happy in the country. If she was not prepared to put up with twenty-four hours of solitude . . .'

'I didn't say she'd left me. It's nothing of that sort. I'm afraid she may have had an accident. Molly went to get her some strawberries, and while she was out Ada went for a stroll in the wood. That was nearly three hours ago, and she hasn't returned.' Jack pulled the bellrope.

'Might she not have walked to the village and—perhaps —been so well amused that she has lost count of the time?'

'Mrs. Harper was in her window as usual; she noted all the comings and goings. Ada didn't go into the village, or to Martland either. She's somewhere in the grounds, and I've got to find her. Oh, there you are, Streeter.' He turned to the elderly butler, and began to explain that he wanted to make up a search-party.

By the time he had issued his orders, Lord Francis was retreating up the stairs.

Jack stared upwards at the slight figure on the half-landing. 'I suppose it is too much to ask you to come and help?'

'I was going to change into some more suitable clothes,' said Francis in a voice of detestable mock-humility. 'Unless you think Ada might consider herself slighted? Do you wish me to ransack the woods for her in full evening dress?'

Jack would have liked to hit him, but decided that this was not a suitable occasion.

There were not many servants at Hoyle Park in its present half-occupied state, but they mustered two footmen and the lamp-boy, as well as three grooms who were round at the stables. All the other outside men and gardeners had gone home. Octavius Barrow stuck his head out of the library, where he was still working on the catalogue in the hopes of being invited to dinner. Jack enlisted him as well. Just as they were leaving the house, they were joined by Lord Francis, now wearing a ditto-suit, a very sporting get-up in which the coat and breeches were made of the same material. Octavius eyed him with envy.

Jack hurried impatiently across the grass, his followers whispering among themselves, for they were not at all sure what was supposed to have happened.

'Excuse me, my lord,' said his personal groom. 'Is there any reason why the young lady must be in the wood, or should we look for her here in the park?'

'It's worth trying, Roberts. You and Hicks can start now, working backwards and forwards from one wall to the other.'

'What about the mausoleum?' suggested Octavius.

'She couldn't have got in there without the key,' said Francis.

The mausoleum was an old Catholic chapel, built above a rather dubious holy spring. After the Reformation, when the villagers had been bullied out of their devotion to the mythical St. Hoya, the Aubrey of those days had converted the chapel into a family burying place.

'The door might have been left open by mistake,' said Jack, uncertainly. 'And if Ada got down into the passage . . .'

'I'll go and make sure she isn't there,' said Francis unexpectedly. 'To set your mind at rest.'

The mausoleum was about fifty yards inside the main gate. Francis turned off in that direction, and the six remaining searchers kept on towards the wood.

It covered about a mile of coastline, and was perhaps half a mile across at its widest point, being unevenly divided by the serpentine course of the Wilderness Walk. The inland sector of the wood was quite flat and regular, but the ground on the far side of the path began to drop away immediately as the headland stooped over the sea. The Wilderness rushed downhill, bearing a torrent of bushes and low, stubby trees, their tentacle-roots fighting for every inch of soil and the spaces between them choked with ivy and brambles and dead timber, and with crevices full of leaves, the broken ground providing a pitfall at every step.

It was easy to stand in the Wilderness Walk and gaze enraptured at the blue silk surface of the sea as it shimmered beyond the interlacing branches, but the actual ground was invisible from above, and if Ada had fallen and lost consciousness somewhere on the headland, the only way to find her was to go and look.

'Come on,' said Jack, pushing ahead of the rest.

For more than an hour they forced their way up and down the steeply tilting ravines of this English jungle, beating through the undergrowth, sweating in the great heat, plagued by flies and midges and all the dry, sharp things that prickle and scratch in dense woodland : twigs and thorns and splinters and bristling thickets of holly. And with all their efforts, they still could not get to the very edge of the cliff, for the land did not break off with the clean edge of a precipice; the bushes and shrubs simply went on clinging to the crumbling earth, far below the point where a man could safely stand.

'She's not here,' said Octavius at last. 'Ten to one the others will have found her by now.' (He had ruined his coat, an elegant creation of his Oxford tailor which had not yet been paid for.)

They climbed painfully back to the comfortable, mossy level of the Wilderness Walk.

'So you had no luck?' said a voice out of the shadows. Francis Aubrey was standing watching them. There was a curious stillness about his posture, as though he might have been there for some time.

Jack's head jerked up. 'The mausoleum?'

'Locked, as I knew it would be.'

'Oh. Then where have you been all this time? Why didn't you come and help us . . .'

'I've been making enquiries. It seems that Mrs. Harper was right; Ada could not have gone into the village and remained so completely unobserved.'

'I still think she's somewhere in there, poor girl.' Jack stared into the heart of the Wilderness.

Octavius said : 'I cannot believe that a girl like Miss Gainey would venture very far into such a labyrinth.'

'No, of course she would not do so. But she might venture a short way and then, losing her balance, fall the rest.'

All the men in the party had played in the Wilderness as children; the lamp-boy played there still, when he could escape from the stern eye of the butler and those insatiable brass lamps. He was twelve years old and a grandson of the lodge-keeper.

He spoke up now, hoarse because he was nervous.

'If a person was to fall, my lord, there'd be something to show for it. Broken branches and such-like.'

'That's very true. If we were to find any traces . . .'

The words trailed off, as Jack grasped the futility of what he was going to say. An hour ago it might have been possible to tell whether Ada had somehow got herself into the thickest part of the Wilderness. Since then, her would-be rescuers had plunged in headlong, obliterating all sign of any presence except their own.

Everyone became suddenly aware of this. It was really quite unnecessary for Francis Aubrey to point the moral. He took great pleasure in doing so, all the same.

They walked back to the cottage, where they were met by Roberts, who reported that there was no lost young lady in the park. The little garden was full of people; Francis's sortie to the village had raised the alarm, Molly had been joined by several of her female relations in a high state of excitement, and a party of tenants and estate workers had volunteered to help in the search, headed by Mr. Sturdy, the steward, a sensible middle-aged man who lived in a house near the Rectory.

It was getting on for eight o'clock but still oppressively close in the small clearing, under the sluggish languor of a sun that seemed as though it was never going to set. The men stood about in clumps, looking solemn and awkward.

One of them was Jem Heard, the young carpenter who had been in the Wilderness that afternoon. Jack began to question him eagerly.

'You must have passed the cottage twice, Jem. Did you happen to see Miss Gainey?'

'I didn't see no one this morning, my lord. Save Molly drawing water from the well. When I wur coming home again I seed the young lady large as life, sat in a chair, not three foot from where I be standing now.'

'Did she speak to you?'

'No, my lord!' exclaimed Jem, gazing at his feudal overlord in a doglike way which would have been very bad for Jack had he not been too worried to notice.

'Did you meet anyone else while you were in the wood?' asked Lord Francis.

'I seed two furriners, my lord. Following along behind me.'

'What sort of furriners, Jem?' asked the village wag. 'Frenchies?'

He was very properly told to mind his manners, this was no time for cutting capers. It was generally understood that a foreigner was merely a visitor, an outsider: in this case the London wine merchant who had mortally offended Sam Roebuck. His good lady, according to Jem, had a bonnet the size of a windmill tied on with red ribbon, and she did laugh a terrible lot. He might not have paid much attention otherwise, for they were about fifty yards behind him. He had reached the village at a quarter past two by the church clock, and spent the rest of the day working at the sawmill under the eye of his father.

'Are you sure you did not meet anyone coming towards you, Jem?' persisted Lord Francis. 'Anyone walking in the direction of Martland?'

Jem shook his head.

'Why do you want to know that?' enquired Jack.

'Because it's the direction Miss Gainey herself must have taken. Either alone or with a companion.'

'That's a lie!' returned Jack, flaring up instantly at the suggestion of a companion. 'We know very well she did nothing of the sort.'

'Just so, my lord,' said Mr. Sturdy, 'but you would do better to come indoors.' Taking his employer's arm, he shepherded him firmly into the cottage.

Francis followed them in. Of the people left in the garden, the only one who counted as gentry was Octavius, and he took this as a sufficient reason for joining this select group in the parlour.

Jack was gazing round the little room that was still full of the presence of the missing girl; there was a book with a paper-knife slipped in it to mark her place, a paisley shawl flung over a chair, an evocation of the scent she always used, faint and teasing.

'Oh, Ada! Why did I ever leave you?' whispered her distracted lover. The sight of his uncle reminded him of the answer to this question. 'You are to blame for this. You let me go off to Alcheston on a wild goose chase, and I shall hold you responsible for whatever may have happened to Ada during my absence.'

'Good God, what a lot of fustian!' said Francis scornfully. He sat down in the most comfortable chair, leant back and closed his eyes. 'What do you suppose can have happened to her?'

'I am afraid she may have fallen from the cliff,' admitted Jack in a low voice, 'and been swept out to sea.'

'Well, that's nonsense to start with. The tide doesn't come in far enough. Anyone who succeeded in falling over

66

the edge of the Wilderness would land on the rocks, and if you think she's done that, you'd better take a boat round and look for her.'

Mr. Sturdy said disapprovingly: 'That is a very heartless way of talking, my lord. I wonder you can be so unfeeling.'

'My dear fellow,' said Francis, opening his eyes again. 'If I thought there was the least likelihood of that young woman lying dead on the rocks, I should not dream of offending your sensibilities. But why are you all besotted with the idea that she has come to grief somewhere on the headland? It seems perfectly plain to me that she must have left by the Martland gate.'

'Well, she didn't,' retorted Jack. 'It was the first thing I thought of, but there was a young lady sittting in the gazebo, and she assured me that no one had come out of the wood during the time that Ada disappeared. No one at all.'

'What sort of a young lady was that? Where did she come from?'

'Miss Prior. She's at the farm . . .'

'*What* name did you say?'

'Prior.' Jack looked at his uncle with a dislike he did not trouble to hide. 'I suppose you recall the family. No one else has ever forgotten your connection with them.'

Francis flushed. 'If you are going to tell me that Lavinia has come down to Devonshire in order to spend the afternoon in our gazebo, I shan't believe you. In any case, she's been married for years.'

'Yes, and she's staying here with her children. It was her sister in the gazebo—Miss Caroline Prior. She seems a sensible girl, and from what she says, I am persuaded that Ada is still somewhere on the estate.'

67

## 9

'Was you intending to take a dip this morning, ma'am?' enquired Mrs. Duffet. 'I hope you may not be inconvenienced by the men down there on the beach.'

'Good gracious, Mrs. Duffet—what men?' asked Lavinia. 'We generally have the whole place to ourselves.'

'They are out looking for the young lady that's disappeared, some of them have been up all night, hacking their way through the Wilderness, and now they think she may be here in Martland after all, and they are searching everywhere, not only the rocks and caves, but in the fields too, and all across the combe and in the lanes. Of course our people have joined in, the work of the farm will have to wait.'

'I heard men's voices calling in the woods last night,' said Caroline. 'But who is it that has disappeared, Mrs. Duffet? It's not by any chance the young lady who is staying at the cottage in the Wilderness?'

'Miss Ada Gainey, that's the one. Vanished from the cottage garden yesterday afternoon and hasn't been seen since. Which some might consider a judgment on her, but I can't help but pity the poor young creature, if she's wandered off and lost her way. She must be very hungry and weary by now.'

'Yes, indeed, poor soul,' said Lavinia.

'Why did you say it was a judgment, Mrs. Duffet?' asked Vinny.

She was the kind of awkward little girl who had a talent for seizing on points that her elders did not wish to discuss.

Caroline created a diversion by lamenting they would have to miss their bathe.

'Why?' demanded the children in unison.

'Well, you would not like a lot of men coming into the cave while we were undressing. It would not be at all the thing.'

'No, because you are ladies,' said Ben. 'At least, you and Mama are ladies and Vinny is just a female. But I am a boy, so I don't care. Mama, can I bathe on my own?'

'No, you can't!' shrieked Vinny. 'You nasty, horrid toad! You won't let him, will you, Mama?'

Caroline managed to separate them before they got to the hair-pulling stage.

At breakfast everyone had something to talk about, even Nurse, who had been woken in the early hours by the sound of shouting and the tramp of heavy feet, so that she forgot the war was over and thought the French had landed.

Presently there was a rap on the front door of the farm-house. The maid answered it, and went flying for her mistress, whom they soon heard, as she hurried along the passage, saying: 'Good morning, my lord. Do pray come in— I fear we are all at sixes and sevens.'

Poor Eltham, thought Caroline. He had already been anxious yesterday outside the wood, by now he must be frantic. She could not help wondering why he had come to the farm.

A few moments later Mrs. Duffet came in, and said, 'Lord Francis would be very much obliged if he could speak to you, miss . . .'

'No!' exclaimed Lavinia. 'I won't—I can't see him. If my husband was here—it's out of the question. He has no business to force himself on me.'

'But it's not you he's asking for, Mrs. Reed. He wants a word with Miss Caroline.'

'With me?' said Caroline. 'Whatever for?'

'I believe it's about something you told the Marquess yesterday, miss. About having seen Miss Gainey at the cottage. They are trying to make out where she can have gone to.'

'Oh. Well, in that case I will certainly tell him all I can, though it isn't very much.'

'You cannot see him, Caro. I—I won't allow it. The whole idea of his coming here is horribly improper.'

Lavinia was shaking with agitation, obsessed by her own fear and dislike of Lord Francis, and apparently indifferent to the emergency which had brought him to the farm. How silly she is, thought her sister impatiently.

'There's nothing for you to worry about, my dear,' she said, getting to her feet. 'This is not a social call. Where have you put him, Mrs. Duffet?'

'He's in the long parlour, miss. There wasn't anywhere else suitable.'

This was a big shabby room that was always let to the summer visitors: it seemed to be full of very old furniture and children's toys. The furniture was polished till it looked as slippery as wet glass. The toys were arranged in neat colonies here and there. Lord Francis Aubrey was standing by the table, inspecting Ben's soldiers.

She had forgotten how small and slight he was—smaller than she had expected, for of course she had grown in the past twelve years, and he hadn't. His face was alert and thin, with a good deal of intelligence but totally undistinguished. He met her without a trace of recognition, and she could not help wondering if he was unaware of ever having seen her before. He had never shown any interest in

Lavinia's younger sister, no doubt considering her beneath his notice.

He apologised civilly enough for disturbing her. 'Did Mrs. Duffet explain the reason for my visit?'

'It is to do with the young lady who has disappeared?'

'Yes. According to what you told my nephew Eltham, it seems that you were the last person to see Miss Gainey.'

'How odd,' said Caroline, perhaps a little fatuously.

'I don't see why,' said Lord Francis, who was not the man to let a foolish remark go unchallenged. 'Someone had to be the last. What I cannot understand is how you persuaded my nephew that she never left the Wilderness. Would you mind repeating to me what you told him?'

Rather stiffly she did so, giving an account of her trip into the wood to find Horace, her glimpse of Ada in the cottage garden, and her return to the combe.

'I remained there until half-past four, and I can assure you that no one came through the wicket-gate during that time except Lord Eltham himself.'

'Oh, come now, Miss Prior—that's rather a sweeping statement. You cannot expect me to believe that you were there for close on two hours and never took your eyes off the wicket-gate.'

'I don't know what I can expect, Lord Francis,' said Caroline rather tartly, 'but there seems very little point in your asking me these questions if you refuse to pay attention to the answers.'

He looked very much surprised, and said, 'I beg your pardon, I did not mean to offend you. But how can you be so absolutely certain? You were playing with the children, perhaps . . .'

'No, I stayed all the time inside the watch-tower—I mean the gazebo. I won't pretend I was always watching the gate, but I would have heard it open and shut. There is quite a loud squeak, you know. And I was on the alert for it; I knew the dog would run off into the wood again, if he got the chance.'

'I see you have made up your mind,' he said, not troubling to hide his annoyance. 'I am sure you have very superior powers of observation, and I suppose this means that you can never bear to admit that you might be mistaken.'

Caroline was not going to be browbeaten.

'I was not mistaken on this occasion,' she said calmly, 'and I cannot imagine why you are so anxious to disbelieve me. What difference does it make to you?'

'To me, none at all. A good deal of difference to Eltham's peace of mind, and perhaps to the safety and comfort of Miss Gainey.'

'I don't understand.'

'Eltham is convinced that she is still somewhere inside the park enclosure; he will not seriously consider looking for her anywhere else. We have now searched the Wilderness three times, and all the open parkland running back to the house. We have investigated the ice-house, the mausoleum and the Roman fountain, though I can't imagine what she would have been doing inside any of them. Eltham has even had himself rowed round the headland in a boat, in case she might have forced her way through the undergrowth and fallen down the side of the cliff. We have not found a trace of her, and I never thought we should. I am perfectly certain that she walked through the wicket-gate into Martland yesterday afternoon, and if it is true that she lost her way on a solitary ramble, she must be in some distress by now—cold, exhausted and possibly injured. Yet it's only this morning that they have started to look for her in this direction. Which is entirely due to you, Miss Prior: to your positive statement that she could not have come through the gate.'

'Oh.' Caroline was for the first moment appalled by this indictment, as though it was her fault that Ada Gainey was still missing.

'I am indeed sorry not to have given you more help, but I *cannot* alter my recollection of what took place. Is it not just as possible that she left by the other gate, the one at the end of the drive?'

'She was not seen there either.'

Caroline knew at once who could have supplied that information. 'I suppose you dare not cast doubts on Mrs. Harper's veracity. Only on mine.'

To her surprise, Francis Aubrey laughed. 'You are right, Mrs. Harper is our informant, and I should not care for the delicate task of pointing out to her that Homer sometimes nods! The fact is, we are not relying on Mrs. Harper alone. If Miss Gainey had walked through Cleave village someone must have noticed her. And no one did.'

Caroline saw the force of that argument. The local people were extremely curious about the London courtesan whom Lord Eltham had installed in Wilderness Cottage. Her sudden appearance in the village street would have aroused great interest and speculation.

In the pause that followed, they both caught the sounds of another man's voice in the hall. Lord Francis turned his head, listening.

'That's Eltham now. Sunk in gloom, poor fellow, and prepared to ask you a great many more questions, I'm afraid.'

Eltham was shown in by an anxious Mrs. Duffet, who wanted to bring him some breakfast, but he refused all offers of tea, ham and eggs, a new, crusty loaf or a bowl of curds and whey. He was not at all pleased to find his uncle already on the premises, and demanded: 'What reason had you to come here?'

'The same as your own, I imagine.'

Caroline was obliged to repeat her story once again. She felt extremely sorry for Eltham, who looked wretched. He was white and drawn, with dark grooves under his eyes. There were smudges of dirt on his coat and a net-work of scratches all over his hands. If Lord Francis had been up all night he had certainly been home to shave and change his shirt. Just as certainly Eltham had not. He made no excuse for his appearance, and this in itself indicated his state of mind, for she was sure he was not naturally boorish or slovenly.

When she had finished her recital, he turned to his uncle, saying: 'There! What did I tell you? Miss Prior knows what she saw—or didn't see. Ada is still somewhere inside the park.'

Lord Francis did not reply (as Caroline half expected) that she was a stupid female who had landed them with this conundrum because she was too conceited, or too pig-headed, to admit she might be wrong. He said, 'There was no one in the gazebo after half-past four. That's when she slipped through.'

'At half-past four?' protested Jack. 'When she'd already been wandering around the wood for two hours, in all that heat? If you suppose she would have set out for a country walk . . .'

'No, of course not. If she'd wanted to go for a walk, she would have passed Miss Prior quite openly in the early afternoon. In fact, I suppose she wanted her departure to be unobtrusive . . .'

'Departure? What the devil do you mean? She wasn't going anywhere. She'd never have gone willingly . . .'

'How do you know? For God's sake, Jack, hold your tongue for a moment, and let me give you the only explanation that I can make any sense of. Suppose Ada decided to leave Devonshire without a lot of fuss. She sent Molly off on a pretext, walked straight out of the cottage and made for the wicket-gate. There she saw Miss Prior in the gazebo and the children playing on the hillside. She waited in the wood for them to go away and when you appeared on the scene she hid among the trees. At last the coast was clear: she descended cautiously into the combe and followed the lane up to the turnpike road, where I think it very likely that she had a friend waiting for her with a carriage.

The end of his theory was almost drowned by Jack's furious protests. It was monstrous to pretend that Ada would have run away. A wicked, cruel, atrocious slander. 'She wouldn't have left me for the world. We love each other, we were blissfully happy . . .'

'So you say. According to the servants, she spent most of her time in tears.'

'That was only because of the awkwardness of her situation.'

Lord Francis remarked that the Gainey sisters had been in the same awkward situation since before Ada was born. 'She must be a doleful sort of girl if she is still crying over spilt milk!'

'What a heartless brute you are!' said Jack wrathfully.

They had forgotten they had an audience. Caroline knew she ought to leave the room. It was shockingly ill-bred, as well as improper, to sit here listening to someone else's family quarrel, but the quarrel itself had blown up so quickly, and there was still something else she felt she ought to point out. She gazed rather helplessly from one Aubrey to the other: from the distracted lover, tall and fair and angry, to the man in the wing-chair, thin and slight and unimpressed—though not unimpressive in his odd way. That scornful expression was what she used to think of as his Richard III face.

'. . . And if she is as mercenary as you pretend,' Jack was saying, 'why did she go creeping off to London just when she had the chance of becoming a marchioness? How do you explain that?'

Lord Francis hesitated. 'She may have thought you were backing out . . .'

'No reason why she should think so. She knew I'd stand by my promise, whatever my family . . . Oh! So that was it! You cunning devil. That's why you induced me to go off on a wild goose chase to Alcheston! You said you'd leave Ada alone, but you never meant to keep your word. All you wanted was a clear field, so that you could coerce and threaten the poor girl, and frighten her into going back to London.'

'This is the wildest nonsense,' began Lord Francis, but Jack paid no attention.

'That's what all your ingenious fairy-tales are about, isn't it? You know she went out by the Martland gate, you know how and when, because you arranged the whole business. She was to disappear without my finding out why—are you going to admit the truth, or shall I have to choke it out of you?'

He launched himself at Lord Francis, who jumped to his feet. He too had become very pale.

'Lord Eltham!' said Caroline at the top of her voice; she had been trying in vain to attract his attention. 'Do

76

please listen to me. What you are saying is quite impossible. It could not have happened.'

'Impossible?'

'It's true there was no one in the gazebo after half-past four, but by that time there was someone in the lane. The two youngest Duffet boys were lopping the branches off that fallen tree—you know where it was, I expect: immediately below the wicket-gate. And afterwards they sawed up the trunk into logs. They were working there until nearly seven, long after you'd begun to search the wood. Mr. Duffet will tell you the same. Miss Gainey could not have been smuggled out through the Martland gate, willingly or otherwise.'

Jack heard her in silence, his hands dropped to his sides.

'Well?' said Lord Francis, straightening his cravat, 'I hope you will now withdraw that list of insults.'

Jack merely shifted his ground. 'I said all along that she was somewhere on the estate. Now you'll have to listen to me.'

## 10

The search for Ada Gainey continued unsuccessfully throughout Wednesday and Thursday, and the deepening mystery hung like a thunder-cloud over the whole village. This had a depressing effect on the holiday party at the farm; Caroline thought that both Lavinia and Nurse were adopting a very timorous attitude, but then Nurse was frightened of the countryside, so large and silent, while Lavinia was simply frightened of encountering Lord Francis. There were to be no more walks or bathes or picnics, everyone must stay within sight of the farm.

'Oh, very well, if it will calm your nerves,' said Caroline, 'but I positively must have something entertaining to read. I'll go into Cleave tomorrow and change our library books.'

This was out of the question. It was not safe for a young woman to walk through the Wilderness; suppose she too was to disappear in broad daylight?'

'You can spare me your Gothic prophecies, my dear. I don't intend to walk. Mr. Duffet has offered to drive me to the village when he goes to Brind Abbas market. It will be hardly a mile out of his way.'

So the following morning Caroline found herself in Cleave with time on her hands. She decided to go first to pay a call on Mrs. Harper, but as she was shown in she discovered that Mrs. Harper had one visitor already.

'It stands to reason she must be dead,' a husky male voice was proclaiming, a voice rich with the overtones of tawny port. 'Or they'd have found her by now. But how am I supposed to act without the verdict of a coroner's inquest behind me?'

Caroline saw a red-faced gentleman of the country sort who almost filled the little room with his presence; she recognised Mr. Joshua Mansard, a local justice of the peace and master of foxhounds—an excessively tedious figure from her childhood, mercifully forgotten ever since.

'Why, my dear Caroline, I was not expecting you,' said Mrs. Harper. She introduced her two callers to each other. Mr. Mansard made Caroline a perfunctory bow; he did not like being interrupted in the full flight of oratory.

'I will come and sit with you a little later, ma'am, if I may,' she said to her hostess. 'I am on my way to the library, and I thought you might like me to change your books for you.'

'Indeed I should, for I am heartily sick of them, I don't know how anyone can publish such stupid stuff, and you may tell Amelia Weatherby so with my compliments. They are over there on the bureau, if you will be good enough to take them.'

While Caroline was collecting the books, Mr. Mansard returned to his discourse, though he seemed to have changed the subject, and she could not immediately see any connection.

'I have never trusted the fellow. He's been sucking the estate dry for years, and God knows where the revenue has gone to, except his own pocket, for he never puts back a penny. He sold all the timber in Lancross Wood because he said the money was needed for improvements, but the devil knows what they were; I never saw any. He simply ruined the best covert in the county, and drove away all my foxes. Did I ever tell you . . .'

'Yes, Joshua, you did,' said Mrs. Harper firmly. 'Several times.'

Caroline slipped out unnoticed, and made her way to the fourth house along the terrace, where she tapped on the open front-door, and was requested, 'please to step in'.

Miss Amelia Weatherby, the proprietress of the library, came into the narrow hall to meet her, and was not deceived by a tactful translation of Mrs. Harper's message.

'Oh dear,' she said, gazing anxiously at Caroline; the bows on her cap stood up in two points, and she looked like a well-meaning rabbit. 'Poor Mrs. Harper is so very hard to please, I was afraid she would not care for . . . but do come in, my dear Miss Prior.'

It was generally thought that Miss Weatherby ran her little lending-library in order to keep herself pleasantly occupied and her house full of chatty neighbours; she could not have made a living out of it, for she provided a much better service than a place like Cleave could actually support. Two break-front bookcases contained her stock-in-trade: three-volume novels bearing the august imprint of John Murray, historical romances, and Gothic tales, as well as essays, poems and books of travel, all neatly arranged according to some system that only Miss Weatherby could understand. The latest periodicals were set out on a table in the window. Being in no hurry, Caroline decided to sit down in comfort and enjoy the pictures of diaphanous dresses and impossibly fashionable hats in *La Belle Assemblée*. There were several people in the room, more interested in gossip than literature, and Caroline had hardly opened her magazine when she was accosted by a lady who had been introduced to her after church last Sunday.

'My dear Miss Prior. you have indeed put a cat among the pigeons! Or a spoke in a certain gentleman's wheel, who thought he was as safe as houses.'

'I'm afraid I don't understand you, ma'am,' said Caroline, astonished by this dazzling array of misplaced metaphors.

Miss North gave a foolish titter. 'Why, if you hadn't been in the gazebo on Tuesday afternoon, that young person's disappearance would have caused very little conjecture. It would have been generally supposed that she had gone back to her old haunts in London. And the truth would never have been known.'

She waited, evidently expecting a reply, but Caroline was still quite mystified and could not think of anything to say. Miss North was beginning to look rather affronted when she was hailed by a friend on the other side of the room.

'Gussie, do pray come here and tell Mr. Richmond what you heard from Octavius.'

Miss North was disappointed in Caroline; she turned away without much ceremony, and was soon absorbed in a conversation with a couple called Phelps, a half-pay captain and his wife, and a young man in riding-dress. They were talking in barely lowered voices, and Caroline could not resist the temptation to listen.

'. . . Not an accidental death, or they must have come across the body by this time . . . Carefully concealed . . . the action of a cool and cunning mind, and who else, I ask you, fills the bill? . . . Very good reason to wish her dead . . . Says he was in the garden, reading, but no one saw him there—none of the men . . . Eltham doesn't believe him either, according to Octavius, but he can hardly say so . . . Family feeling . . .'

So that was how they had solved the mystery. They thought that Ada had been killed deliberately, and that Francis Aubrey was her murderer.

His motive, if they were right, was a sordid one. He was Lord Eltham's trustee, and there were rumours that he had been speculating with his nephew's capital; the unexpected winding-up of the Trust at this juncture might have meant his utter ruin and disgrace. And the Trust was to end when Eltham married; the fact that he was contemplating such a rash and unsuitable marriage would have made the prospect even more bitter.

Everyone seemed to know about Lord Francis's extravagance—he had spent a fortune on his collection of Chinese porcelain—and the love of money (perhaps a desperate need for money) which had hardened him against all other considerations.

'Just think of the way he behaved to that young lady he was engaged to,' said Mrs. Phelps, a fading blonde. 'When he found out that she wasn't going to be an heiress after all, he threw her over without a qualm—left her standing at the church door on her wedding day, I believe. They say the poor creature went into a decline.'

Caroline was surprised to recognise her sister as the heroine of this affecting story. She had not realised that Francis Aubrey's treatment of Lavinia was still so widely (if inaccurately) remembered and held against him.

'It is all very dreadful,' said Miss Weatherby, who was hovering about, apparently polishing the spines of the library books. 'One would not suppose that a member of the nobility—yet I cannot think well of a man who is prepared to cut down all those beautiful trees. First Lancross Wood and now the Wilderness.'

'The Wilderness?' they all exclaimed. 'You cannot be serious?'

'Oh yes, it is quite true. Lord Francis told me so himself. I met him in the village, on Tuesday morning, I think it was. "Oh, my lord," I said, "what a pity it is that you had to cut down the fine old trees in Lancross Wood, what will you be doing next?" And he replied immediately, "I am selling the timber in the Wilderness, Miss Weatherby; that's next on the list." And he did not sound as if he cared in the least.'

There was an outburst of indignation. The most sensible comment came from the young man in riding-dress, whose name was Mr. Richmond. 'He won't get much from that transaction. The trees there are hardly worth felling.'

'He must be in dire straits,' said Captain Phelps. 'Wants every penny he can lay hands on. Well, he's a gamester. All that family are; the late Marquess was notorious.'

Caroline felt strangely depressed. She made a selection of library books, and returned with her spoils to the house on the corner.

82

Mrs. Harper was now alone. She glanced over the books with a disparaging eye, said she had read two of them already, and asked whom Caroline had seen at Miss Weatherby's.

'Charles Richmond is Joshua Mansard's godson,' she remarked. 'And probably his heir. They rode down this morning from Brind, and poor Mansard is in a great state of agitation, as you may have noticed, for he takes his duties as a magistrate very seriously, and he is aware that he ought to do something about the disappearance of this young woman, but he cannot determine precisely what.'

'They were saying in the library that Lord Francis Aubrey has murdered her.'

'They are saying it all over the countryside, I collect.'

'But, ma'am—do you think him capable of such a dreadful crime?'

'In certain circumstances. Suppose he had met the little hussy in the wood—either by chance or design—and she taunted him, knowing her power over Jack. She might have driven him too far. He had a very violent temper as a young man.' Mrs. Harper was silent for a moment. Then she said: 'I'll tell you one thing. If he killed the girl by accident, he wouldn't lose his head. I think it more than likely he would hide the body in some ingenious place where no one else could find it.'

'And this is the man my parents chose as a husband for Lavinia,' said Caroline. 'No wonder she was afraid of him.'

'It would have been a disastrous marriage, I thought so at the time. Mind you, I'm not saying Francis got rid of Ada Gainey, but it seems as though someone must have done, and he was bound to be suspected. He is not much liked.'

'It is hardly surprising.'

The old lady sat with her stiff hands folded, contemplating the past.

'He was a puny little fellow,' she said at last. 'No one thought he would survive his infancy. He always looked like a changeling among those handsome Aubreys, but he had to keep up with the rest of them, just the same, for his father made no concessions. He had no use for weaklings. I can see Francis now, at twelve years old, struggling to mount a horse that was too big for him. He couldn't get his foot in the stirrup. And the old lord was mocking him, while Dillingford, the eldest son, sat there grinning. Yet Francis had twice the brains of his brother Dill.'

Again Caroline was reminded of Richard III. She could not have been such a perceptive little girl, when she first saw Lord Francis, that she had grasped the similarity all on her own. More likely she had picked up the idea from overhearing a grown-up conversation. The clever, sickly, resentful younger son, transformed into a wicked uncle.

Mrs. Harper was beginning to tire, and Caroline decided she must bring her visit to an end. She would walk up and meet Mr. Duffet on the main road, and save him the necessity of driving down into the village.


## II


As the lane from the village climbed higher, the trees became fewer, the sun grew harsher and brighter, and at the top where the steep banks ended there was quite a rough wind, in spite of the heat, which blew about in little nagging spurts of dust and grit. The place where the lane joined the turnpike road was featureless, there was no shade and nowhere to sit.

Caroline decided that she could not wait on this bleak corner for Mr. Duffet, who might not arrive for another hour. She retraced her steps towards the village. She did not know what to do next. She could not return to Mrs. Harper's comfortable drawing-room, for she was sure the old lady needed a respite from visitors, and she was not on calling terms with anyone else in Cleave. As she reached the closed gates of Hoyle Park she gazed longingly in at the refreshing sight of emerald-green grass and deep leafy trees, and wished she had not given Lavinia a ridiculous promise to stay out of the Wilderness. She could so easily have walked back to the farm. Well, surely it would do no harm if she ventured just inside the park? There was a rustic bench where she could sit for a while in peace, and no one could possibly attack her within earshot of the lodge. She pushed the door in the wall and stepped resolutely through into the arcadian world of the Wilderness.

It was very pleasant in the shelter of the trees, with the birds singing continuously overhead. Caroline did not sit down on the bench, she walked some way along the edge of the wood, and presently came to a small stone building with narrow pointed windows: the chapel belonging to the mediaeval holy well and later converted by the Aubreys into a family mausoleum.

This place had haunted Caroline's imagination when she was a child with a kind of delicious terror, but she had never been inside, for it was always locked. Today she was surprised to find that the weathered oak door was slightly open. As she stood there, the crack widened and a man came out. It was Francis Aubrey.

Caroline was about twenty yards from the building, and

as luck would have it there was a beech tree just in front of her. She froze into the landscape, hardly daring to breathe, while all the things she had heard and thought about Lord Francis came rushing into her mind. For a moment she was sure he had seen her—he seemed to be staring straight at her—but his gaze travelled on and his expression did not change. He looked carefully to left and right, he seemed to be listening too. Then he tiptoed cautiously round the chapel, as though to make certain that there was no one lying in wait on the other side. After which he set off across the park with the same furtive, catlike tread.

He must have been completely obsessed by the fear of being seen, for he left the door unfastened, with the key in the lock.

Caroline stood there, trying to make sense of this episode. Could Ada's body be hidden in the mausoleum? There was a horrid aptness in the idea. Or perhaps—she remembered that there was supposed to be a smugglers' passage that ran up from the seashore and came out somewhere near the well.

As though drawn by an invisible string, she went into the chapel.

The interior was orderly and clean, the rough-cast walls being lined with gracefully inscribed memorials. There were some elegant tombs, dwarfed by the centre-piece: an alabaster lady and gentleman, with alabaster cutlet frills round their necks, lying on a hideous erection of black marble which looked like a four-poster bed.

Caroline was in no mood to admire antiquities. She put down her heavy basket of books and went over to examine the so-called well—it was really a spring—whose water bubbled out below the bare stone altar and ran into a lead-lined basin rather like a font. This basin was set in a small chamber several feet below the floor of the chapel, and the constant overflow of water ran away through a stone archway in the subterranean wall. There were some steps leading to this lower level. Caroline went down them and tried unsuccessfully to peer through the arch. After a slight hesitation, she stooped nearly double and sidled herself through, taking care not to wet her feet, which was not difficult for there was only a thin trickle of water.

Straightening up carefully on the other side of the arch, she found it was possible to stand upright. She was in a man-made tunnel, about three feet wide and six feet high, shored up with wooden beams and probably adapted out of the bed of a submerged stream. The stream itself ran along in a channel beside the footpath. The air was dank and the tunnel dim and shadowy, though not as dark as she would have expected, and on looking upwards, she saw a narrow shaft in the roof which provided light and ventilation.

Caroline walked on down the passage, her mind full of excited speculations. There was an overhead ventilator every few yards, though some of these were choked with leaves, and it was in one of the unlighted patches that she suddenly became aware of a strong waft of scent.

She stopped and sniffed, incredulous at first, but then convinced. She wasn't dreaming, she really could smell expensive French scent.

Suppose Ada was still alive, somewhere in the tunnel?

'Is there anyone there?' called Caroline. 'Can you hear me?'

No reply. She hurried on. The smugglers' passage seemed to stretch on for ever (how far was it from the chapel to the shore?). The scent was still in her nostrils.

It was then that she heard the tapping. Faintly at first, because of the chortle of the stream, but quite distinctly, an uneven tap-tap, tap! pitiful little sounds, as though someone was weakly trying to attract attention. A prisoner who could not move or shout, and who had perhaps been down here for three nights and two days.

She began to run. The passage took an abrupt turn and she came to a halt, staring. She had reached the end of the secret way. A shallow cave lay ahead of her, and beyond it she had a clear view of rocks and sea. The sun was streaming in from the south, so that the whole of the cave was bathed in daylight, and it was absolutely empty. There was no bound figure, no imprisoned beauty anywhere to be seen. Though she could still hear the tapping.

She stepped out of the cave. There was no sand or shingle on this beach, just a chaotic jumble of huge boulders, and beyond them the sabre-edged lines of flat rock jutting between the land and the sea. This was part of the headland, below the Wilderness and between the two bays; the cliff shelved down in a sort of landslide, with shrubs and bushes straggling over like a green cascade, and as she looked round at the cave Caroline saw a spindly branch, right over the entrance, knocking fitfully backwards and forwards in the wind.

So that was where the tapping had come from. She stood on the beach annoyed with herself for having been so gullible, and it then struck her that she had spent a good deal of time pursuing this fantasy; she must get back to the village to meet Mr. Duffet. As soon as she went back into the tunnel she was assailed by the pungent French scent.

Ada had been here at some time or other, that at least seemed certain. Caroline made her way up the enclosed

88

passage wondering what she ought to do about her suspicions. Preoccupied, she reached the chapel, retrieved her basket, and lifted the latch of the door. Nothing happened. She pressed the latch harder and pushed. It took her several seconds to realise that she was locked in.

She was so astonished that at first she felt simply indignant, rattling at the handle and looking through each of the leaded windows in turn to see if there was anyone outside who could come and set her free. But all she could see through the dusty glass was a vista of grass and trees. It had never struck her that Lord Francis might come back to the mausoleum and lock the door. Of course he could not have known she was inside—or could he? Her basket had been plainly exposed, right at the foot of the marble four-poster. A shiver of apprehension ran up her spine. Although Ada was not in the smugglers' passage now, it seemed to have some vital connection with her disappearance, and anyone who discovered so much might be in danger of sharing the same fate. It would be madness to stay here in the chapel, like a mouse in a trap.

She would have to go back to the beach and make her escape from there. She had heard the young Duffets say that you could go from Martland to Cleave along the seashore, if you didn't mind some hard going. Caroline was well-shod and rather enjoyed clambering about the rocks. She set off once again down the tunnel, this time carrying the basket.

The strip of shore in front of the cave was bounded on either side by a buttress of cliff thrusting out towards the sea and cutting off any extensive view of the coast. Caroline knew, from the position of the mausoleum itself, that she could not be very far from Cleave; the little harbour with its fishing-boats was probably just round the corner of the tall cliff on her left. She set off diagonally, with that cliff as her goal.

She could not go very fast; the gigantic hurly-burly of stones made walking awkward for a girl in a long, narrow skirt; the stones were so big and set at such random angles, it was difficult to step from one to the other, especially if you were carrying a heavy basket. It took her longer than she expected even to get as far as the proper rocks, and they were worse to walk over, with their broken surfaces and treacherous patches of weed.

Caroline plodded on, head down, watching where she was going. The tide was coming in, the waves crashing lustily on the rocky escarpment and throwing up splinters of spray. Twice she stopped, changed the basket on to her other arm, and looked longingly at that tantalising piece of cliff which never seemed to get much nearer.

The third time she looked up, she got a fright that jerked her heart into her throat. Francis Aubrey had just rounded the corner of the cliff and was heading straight towards her.

At this moment Caroline gave way to panic. She turned wildly and began to run in the opposite direction. He was shouting at her. She could not distinguish the words above the noise of the sea, but his voice sounded angry and threatening. Caroline stumbled from rock to rock, jarring her feet and twisting her ankles. Where was she to go? Not back into that dreadful tunnel. Her only hope was to get round the other corner, round the tip of the headland, into Martland Mouth. But it was too far, he was gaining on her fast; he would catch her long before she got there.

She was still stupidly clutching the basket; she dropped it and was thankful to be rid of the weight. Breathless, she pounded on, over the endless ridges of rock. She saw the bright streak of weed, but it was too late; her foot shot off the rim of slime—she recovered, tripped and slammed down on to her hands and knees, half-stunned by the impact.

She tried to drag herself up. Her pursuer's shadow slid over her like a noose; she could almost feel him standing above her.

'Do you want to break your neck?' enquired Lord Francis. He did not sound sinister, merely exasperated. 'What possessed you to run off in that lunatic fashion—did you imagine I was going to abduct you as well?'

'As—as well?' she faltered.

'I'm supposed to have abducted the little Gainey—it's all over the village . . . Good God, that's exactly what you did think! My dear Miss Prior, I am sorry if I alarmed you, but how could you be so silly?'

She sat up on the rock, nursing her bruises, and they gazed at each other. He was apparently amused, but not unkindly so. There was so much humour in that thin, clever face—it seemed impossible that it should be the face of a murderer. All the same, there was a lot that needed expaining.

'You locked me in the chapel,' she protested. 'And you came down here and shouted at me . . .'

'I shouted with good reason. You don't want to be drowned, do you?'

'What do you mean?'

'The tide's coming in. Had you not noticed?'

She stared around her. The beach had been foreshortened, most of the barren rocks had disappeared under the blue sweep of the sea. The foot of the cliff which she had been aiming to reach was now several feet deep in water, with great waves slapping over the hidden boulders, and a strong current running.

'Oh! I did not think . . .'

'It is dangerous to get caught. In fact we shall have to move from here. Do you feel sufficiently recovered?'

He held out his hands to help her up. Caroline let him do so without any sense of reluctance. She now saw that the sea-water was rushing ahead of them along all the gulleys between the rocks, swirling over miniature waterfalls and filling stone-bound pools, so that they were walking across a string of tiny islands. They came to a place where the surrounding water was too wide for her to step across. She was tired, as well as being shaken by her fall; she hung back, uncertainly.

'Put your arm round me,' said Lord Francis. 'So.' And without more ado, he hoisted her up and carried her across the chasm in one stride.

Although he was so small and slight, he must be extremely strong, for he did not give her the least feeling that he might drop her in the sea. When he put her down she noticed that he was about an inch shorter than she was, though very well proportioned, wiry and resilient.

'There,' he said. 'You are safely back on dry land.'

The beach had been reduced to a small patch in front of the cave.

'Is it high tide yet?' she asked.

He looked at his watch. 'Five minutes to go. You will have to put up with my company for the next hour, until we can walk round the point, so we may as well be as comfortable as we can. Would you care to sit behind this rock out of the sun?'

Caroline noticed that something was missing. 'Oh—my basket! The library books!' She gazed frantically out to sea.

'I'm afraid the fish are reading them by now.'

'Oh dear, what am I to say to Miss Weatherby?'

'Why not tell her the truth? It has all the properties of a bad novel.'

This was horribly embarrassing. She thought Lord Francis had probably saved her life; this was no logical reason for abandoning her suspicions, but the fact was that they now seemed ludicrous and impertinent. She felt that she ought to apologise for them, but did not know how.

He was watching her with a certain ironic sympathy. 'It wasn't entirely your fault,' he said. 'I did lead you on.'

She stared at him, a new idea growing in her mind.

'When you came out of the mausoleum, did you know I was there?'

'My dear girl, I could not fail to know. You do not become invisible simply by standing behind a tree. Or transparent. And you looked so dramatic, I could not resist giving the sort of performance you seemed to require. I must be a better actor than I thought—I had no idea you would take my little charade so seriously.'

Caroline felt every kind of fool.

'You intended me to explore the passage. You locked me in.'

'No, that was an accident, I assure you. I had better tell you the whole story. You know why that passage was built, I suppose? For the convenience of the free-traders. This was done at a time when the family was not often in Devonshire. We don't much care to have our ancestors' burial-place used to store contraband, and the practice has almost ceased, but occasionally they still bring in a cargo. On Tuesday night, when we were searching for Ada we found traces of a fairly recent visit. There was a lot of debris—one of the cases must have split open when they were dragging them across the rocks at low tide—and there was broken glass and sawdust everywhere, not only in the passage but in the chapel itself. I told one of the gardeners to get the stuff cleared away, and this morning I went to make sure this had been done and found the whole place in good order but smelling like a—that is to say, the air is heavily scented. I fancy they must have stumbled on an unbroken bottle in the sawdust, and then broken it.'

Caroline stirred involuntarily, but did not speak.

'Of course you must have noticed the scent. Did you suppose you were on the brink of rescuing the fair Ada?' He really was fiendishly acute. 'Poor Miss Prior! What would you have thought if the passage had been reeking of brandy?'

'I expect I should have thought you were a secret tippler, Lord Francis,' said Caroline, refusing to be crushed.

She was immediately conscious of the impropriety of such a retort—especially to a man who was almost old enough to be her father.

Lord Francis did not mind. His eyes lit up with laughter, it was astonishing how this changed his whole countenance. 'That's about the only sin I haven't been accused of. Well, it was after this prosaic errand that I caught sight of you lurking behind your tree. I ought not to have teased you as I did. My excuse is that I meant to return immediately and set your mind at rest, but I was summoned to the cottage, where they were about to send a man down the well . . .'

'Good heavens, they did not find anything, I hope?'

'No, of course not. I knew they would not. However, that wasted some time, and when I got back to the mausoleum I discovered some well-meaning busybody had locked the door and removed the key. I called your name several times, and since you did not answer it struck me that you might be down here already trying to make your way across the rocks. I was afraid you would be caught by the tide.'

'And so I should have been,' said Caroline soberly. She looked out towards the mass of water that was tossing and swelling round the base of the cliff. 'I am very grateful to you, sir.'

'Then will you do something for me in return? Will you tell me why it has been generally decided that I am the villain who has made away with Ada Gainey?'

Caroline was tongue-tied. She could not think what to say. In the end she stammered something about his being thought to have a plausible motive.

'To prevent Jack from rushing into a marriage he is bound to regret? Or because I am determined to retain my hold on the family purse-strings? No one could possibly suppose that either of those reasons was sufficient.'

Caroline did not feel able to disillusion him.

'The fact is,' he said, 'that the local gentry dislike me, though I don't know what I have done to earn their ill-will. I believe my manner is not conciliating . . .'

At this point Caroline disgraced herself again. She laughed out loud, she could not help it.

The little man glared at her. 'What have I said to amuse you, Miss Prior?'

'Oh, nothing, Lord Francis. Nothing at all.'

He continued to look fierce, but she was beginning to take his measure by now, so she gazed steadily back, and he soon gave in and smiled.

'Well, I suppose I have got a sharp tongue, but I never did any harm to a living soul in these parts—excepting old Mansard, who persists in thinking I cut down Lancross Wood entirely to annoy his foxes.'

She remembered Mrs. Harper's story of the young Francis struggling to get on a horse that was too big for him; perhaps he had ended by hating the normal pursuits of his class.

'Do you not hunt yourself, sir?'

He seemed surprised. 'Naturally I hunt. In Leicestershire.'

Which must add insult to injury, as far as the Devonshire sportsmen were concerned, but apparently he did not see this.

'The very notion of trees being felled is repugnant to many people,' she said after a moment's hesitation. 'I know it is sometimes necessary, but when I hear you were preparing to cut down the Wilderness . . .'

'Cut down the Wilderness! What nonsense is this? Where did you hear such a preposterous rumour?'

'It isn't true, then?'

'Of course not. I should be just as likely to cut off my own head.'

'How very strange. Miss Weatherby said that you told her yourself . . .'

'Miss Weatherby?' he exclaimed in a different tone. Do you mean to say that goose of a woman actually repeated—what are you laughing at now, Miss Prior?'

'You did tell her, didn't you? Just to see how much she would swallow?'

'She kept fluttering round,' he said defensively. ' "Oh, Lord Francis, what will you do next?" So I thought of the most improbable thing I might do next and gave her that for an answer.'

'You don't suffer fools gladly, do you?' She was beginning to think that this, together with an undisciplined sense of humour, might be the real reason for his unpopularity.

96

'I don't suffer them at all, if I can help it. What sensible man does?'

'Not many gentlemen of your station in life, I dare say. Most men and nearly all women are obliged to put up with a certain amount of folly as a matter of expediency.'

'Is that your own experience?' He looked at her in a new way, as though suddenly recalling who she was. 'I believe your parents are no longer living. Do you make a permanent home with your sister?'

'With my sister and brother-in-law,' she said stiffly.

'I hope he is not one of the fools you are suffering gladly.'

'He is a most excellent man.' It was intolerable to have Lavinia's husband sneered at by the man who had treated Lavinia so badly, and just because Caroline was often irritated by Arthur she felt obliged to exaggerate. 'It is a charming household; I am very happy with them, and very fortunate . . .' She caught his look of polite scepticism and finished, rather lamely : 'There are no more inconveniences than one is bound to meet with in sharing someone else's home.'

'There is a remedy. You should get married.'

'That is not so easy for a woman with no fortune.'

Directly she had spoken, she realised that this remark had a very personal application. She glanced sideways at Francis Aubrey; he had flushed with mortification, and it was plain that her words had stung. She was surprised to find him so vulnerable. Perhaps he had always been ashamed of having jilted Lavinia. When a man took such an irrevocable step, it was difficult to grasp the fact that he might regret it almost immediately.

There was a long silence. Francis stooped to pick up a pebble which he flung into the sea. The tide had started to recede but the foot of the cliff was still submerged; they would have to spend a little longer in their desert-island isolation.

To break the spell, she asked: 'What do you yourself think has happened to that poor girl?'

'I have not the smallest doubt that she is back in Mount Street by now, in the bosom of her precious family.' He had recovered his usual composure.

'But surely—if she was expecting to marry Lord Eltham —why should she run away?'

'The marriage was by no means a certainty. Eltham is not at all the man to go against the wishes of his mother and sisters, no matter what he may pretend. The affair would never have come to this stage if Lady Eltham had been in London, instead of in Scotland dancing attendance on Lucy, and once all his womenfolk had united in condemning the engagement, he would have begun to waver. I dare say young Miss Gainey was shrewd enough to recognise this. I think her flight is part of a policy of teasing and tormenting him, in order to strengthen the hold she has over him. The stranglehold of infatuation.'

This seemed to Caroline an odd, roundabout way of capturing a husband, but it was not her business to argue with a man who knew a great deal more about the world than she did. Except on one point that she felt strongly about.

'You haven't explained how Ada managed to leave Hoyle Park without being seen.'

'You must not ask me that. I shall start to be unconciliating once again.'

'You still think she came through the wicket-gate.'

He was not to be drawn.

Caroline had an inspiration. 'Might she not have found

the door of the mausoleum open, as I did, and come down the passage?'

'What difference if she had? She would have had to walk through either Cleave or Martland to reach the turn-pike road. We are all agreed that she could not have gone through Cleave without being noticed, and as for Mart-land—surely you would have seen her from the gazebo? A girl in white, appearing suddenly on the beach, as though she had risen from the waves?'

'I did not mean—I was wondering whether she might have been drowned.'

'The sea was right out on Tuesday afternoon,' he re-minded her. 'Miss Prior, you must not distress yourself by brooding on these dreadful possibilities. I intend to go to London as soon as I can, to solve the mystery once for all —I am waiting only for my niece Anne to arrive from Somerset, so that she can keep an eye on Jack while I am away . . . I think the tide has gone down far enough for us to walk round the point. Shall we go and see?'

As they made their way over the boulders, they caught sight of the library basket, lodged in a crevice between two rocks. Francis went to fetch it. The straw was dark and pulpy, the soaking wet books were heavy and stained with salt. Runnels of water poured through every gap in the straw. He insisted on bringing this pathetic object along with them, in spite of her protests.

'You can get Mrs. Duffet to dry the books in front of the kitchen fire.' He held the basket in front of him as though it was a watering-pot.

With the tide only just off them, the rocks shone as though they had been polished: the sea, no longer a men-ace, sparkled at a safe distance. Caroline and Francis walked round the end of the cliff on to the grey shingle of Cleave beach. There were some fishermen sitting on an upturned boat, mending their nets; they gazed at his lordship and the young lady with unbridled curiosity.

The village seemed uncommonly full of people standing about and talking excitedly, among them Octavius Barrow and Miss Weatherby. Caroline was wondering whether there was some fresh news of Ada when she realised that she herself was the focus of attention. Several people cried, 'Here she is,' and a complete stranger shook her head and said, 'Thank God you are safe!'

At this moment she saw Mr. Duffet's gig, with Lavinia sitting in it, as white as chalk and clutching a vinaigrette.

'Caro!' shrieked Lavinia. 'Where have you been? We all thought you were dead.'

It dawned on Caroline that she had inadvertently become another Vanishing Young Lady. She must have been seen entering the Wilderness about two hours ago, after which she had disappeared as completely as Ada Gainey.

'I am so sorry, my dear,' she said, feeling rather guilty but speaking as lightly as possible. 'I stupidly got myself locked in the chapel, and was obliged to leave by way of the covered passage.'

This aroused a good deal of interest. Two figures bore down on them through the crowd: Mr. Joshua Mansard, looking portentous, and Octavius's father, old Canon Barrow, looking grave.

'Well, Aubrey—what were you doing on the headland?' demanded Mr. Mansard. 'How do you account for your presence?'

'Lord Francis very kindly came to my rescue,' said Caroline, quickly, because she thought he was about to make some provoking reply.

Lavinia was visibly ignoring her former suitor. 'I told

you not to go into the Wilderness,' she said plaintively to Caroline. 'I have been half out of my mind with worry, ever since Mr. Duffet came back to the farm and said you had disappeared, just like that unfortunate girl.'

'Well, I have said I'm sorry, and for goodness' sake let us go home. Mr. Duffet, I do beg your pardon for being such a nuisance.'

Mr. Duffet said placidly that he was happy to be of service.

Caroline got into the gig, and Francis stepped forward with the basket.

'Good morning, Mrs. Reed,' he said civilly.

'Good morning, sir,' said Lavinia in a die-away voice. 'Oh—what is that?'

'Your library books, ma'am.' He deposited his dripping burden at her feet.

Buffoon, thought Caroline. As they drove off she caught a glimpse of Miss Weatherby looking scandalised. She wondered what sort of a fairy-story Lord Francis would regale her with this time.

## 12

Francis Aubrey drove into London about two o'clock on Monday, the twenty-fifth of June, having spent a day and a half on the road. (He had no scruples about Sunday travelling.) He went straight to Albany, changed his clothes, and then walked through the Mayfair squares to that impudently respectable house in Mount Street. There was a thick layer of straw spread across the road outside, to deaden the sound of passing carriages : a sign that some-one in the house was seriously ill. Francis rapped on the door. Nothing happened. He rapped again, more loudly.

The door was opened, not by the usual smart footman, but by a female in a crumpled apron, who announced: 'They ain't receiving no visitors.'

'They are going to receive me!' said Francis, sticking his foot in the doorway before she had time to shut him out. 'Kindly inform Miss Ada Gainey that Lord Francis Aubrey desires to speak to her without delay.'

The maid gave a yelp of horror, shrinking back against the wall. Then she fled upstairs, leaving the front door open.

Francis stepped into the hall. It had the feeling of a place where ordinary life had broken down, the floor was unswept, and the silver candelabra on a small side-table were tarnished, with rivulets of wax drooping from their burnt-out stumps. A door on the right led to the dining-room. Francis looked in. A man with a dissipated, melancholy face was drinking brandy from a tumbler. He blinked stupidly.

'Are you the doctor?'

'Do I look like the doctor?' snapped Francis.

'How should I know? They keep me in the dark, they don't tell me . . .'

Several people were coming down the stairs. A golden virago in a figured muslin dress was talking at the top of her voice.

'Just let me see the monster, that's all! Coming here to gloat over us . . .'

'Betsey, do for heaven's sake try not to fly into a passion!' begged one of her companions, a tall man in the uniform of a colonel of hussars.

Betsey Gainey had caught sight of Francis by this time.

'How dare you show your face here, you viper? Sending insolent messages . . .'

'I sent no message to you, ma'am. My business is with your youngest sister. I am sorry if you have illness in the house . . .'

'Oh, sorry, is it? When you have killed my sister, and done your best to kill my mother . . .'

'Betsey, you haven't a shred of evidence,' said Colonel Corbet.

'Let me speak to Lord Francis.' Sally Gainey came down the last few steps, brushing past her sister. 'I am sure the servant did not understand you, sir. Have you perhaps brought us news of Ada?'

'Is she not here with you?'

'No, how could she be? You must know that your nephew wrote on Wednesday morning to tell us that Ada was missing—and apart from that we know only what we have read in the newspaper. Why should you come looking for her here?'

'I thought she might have made her way back to London by this time.'

'I never heard such cold-blooded effrontery,' burst out Betsey.

'Pray do not trifle with us, my lord.' Sally gazed at him with her large beautiful eyes. 'I beg of you, tell us what you have done with Ada. I cannot believe you have actually taken her life, no matter what it says in the public prints. If only you will set her free, I promise she will not make any further claims on your nephew.'

'My dear Miss Sally, I assure you . . .'

'The case is urgent, you see, on account of my poor mother. She was greatly shocked by Lord Eltham's letter—

though only believing Ada to have been lost all night in the woods—but after we saw the account in the *St. James Chronicle* she suffered an apoplectic seizure and is now extremely ill.'

'I am very sorry to hear it, but if you think I have had anything to do with your sister's disappearance, you are quite mistaken. I don't know what the public prints have got hold of . . .'

'They say you are a murderer, and that everyone knows it,' stated Betsey.

'These are two of my daughters,' remarked the brandy-drinker, shuffling across from the dining-room. 'Whores, both of them. All my five daughters are whores. Did you know that, sir?'

Francis opened his mouth and shut it again. For the first time in years he denied himself the pleasure of saying exactly what came into his head.

'And now some scoundrel has carried off my dear little Ada, the only one who wasn't ashamed of her old father.'

'Do hold your tongue, Papa,' said Betsey.

Colonel Corbet suggested that perhaps Lord Francis would care to tell them what steps were being taken to find Ada.

'Yes, certainly. And I should also like to know what I myself am accused of.'

Mr. Gainey had returned to the brandy-bottle. The rest of the party went upstairs to the drawing-room, where a newspaper, dated Friday the twenty-second, was thrust into Francis's hand.

The paragraph was phrased in the usual unctuous language, with a travesty of discretion which anyone could penetrate.

'*A shocking event took place lately at the Devonshire*

*seat of a certain noble Marquess. His lordship having with-
drawn from town to enjoy the company of the beautiful
Miss . . . (youngest of that troop of sisters who are so famous in the neighbourhood of Mount Street for their obliging
frailty) the happy couple were pursued to their amorous
retreat by the Marquess's uncle, Lord . . . who has taken
such a close interest in his nephew's inheritance that he
dare not contemplate resigning the powers of a Trustee.
On the very day after the Marquess had announced his
intention of marrying his fair Cyprian, she vanished in the
most mysterious circumstances. Since this Disappearance
took place within the confines of . . . Park, and since no
living person could have left the estate unobserved, it is
feared that the young woman must have fallen a victim,
in the full bloom of her youth, to the ruthless cupidity
of her lover's near relative and heir.'*

'I have never read such an atrocious catalogue of lies!'
exclaimed Francis when he had finished this effusion.

No one spoke. They just stood there, watching him.
He glanced from one to the other, as though he was unable
to credit their combined hostility.

The two remaining sisters had quietly entered the room:
Hester Gainey and Celia Page, the one who had married
and hardly ever came near her family. She was pregnant and
beginning to lose her looks. The beautiful Hester was
showing her thirty-four years. Her face was drawn and
sleepless, her clear skin blotched with crying. Her shoulders slumped a little wearily, so that her body was no longer as taut and graceful as it had been.

She looked at Francis, and asked in a dull voice: 'What
have you done with her?'

'I haven't done anything. For God's sake, Hester—surely
*you* don't believe this nonsense?'

'It's what you threatened. You said you would get rid of her, and you have.'

'Well, you don't imagine I meant—anything of this kind?'

'What did you mean?'

He stared at her with a baffled expression, but did not answer.

Sally asked: 'Then what do you yourself suppose has happened to Ada, sir?'

'I don't know. I haven't considered the matter. To tell you the truth, I was convinced she had got tired of rusticating and come back here. She did not like Devonshire, you know.'

'She was prepared to endure it,' said Hester. 'I'll read you a passage from her last letter.'

'And could we not sit down?' he suggested. 'After all, we are not performing an opera.'

The fiery Betsey said something scathing about his lordship's manners, but Hester, his former mistress, smiled faintly, and said: 'You don't change, do you, Francis?'

Then she became grave once more, fetched a letter from the bureau and came to sit beside him on the sofa.

'This is dated a week ago last Sunday, two days before she disappeared. Here we are . . . "*I do not at all like this cottage, it is so dark that I feel quite smothered by the trees, and the branches creak all night . . .*" '

'What did I tell you?'

'Listen to how she goes on. "I shall not have to live like this much longer, for today my dear Eltham put all his hints and meanings into words and made me an offer of marriage, and I am sure he will stick to his promise, whatever his friends may say. I dare say I shall grow used to living in the country. I find Eltham has three different estates, of which Hoyle Park is the smallest, as well as the London house and a hunting-box at Melton." This is not very much to the point,' commented Hester, with a touch of embarrassment. She skipped a few lines. ' "The more I see of E. the more I like him. He is kind and generous and honourable, besides being extremely handsome and agreeable. He will make a charming husband . . . !" There! You can see she had no intention of leaving him—not even as a temporary stratagem, to inflame his passion and bring him up to scratch, which I fancy is what you had in mind, my dear Francis.'

He accepted this thrust with unusual docility, and his voice was merely puzzled as he admitted: 'She certainly does not sound as though she meant to run away.'

'Poor little Ada,' whispered Sally, her eyes filling with tears.

'In any case,' said Celia, 'I do not see how she could have left him. Willingly, I mean. According to what Eltham wrote to Hester, Hoyle Park is entirely surrounded by high walls and inaccessible cliffs, and the only two gates are under constant supervision. Is that correct, Lord Francis?'

'To all intents and purposes, yes. Both were overlooked by witnesses on that particular afternoon.' He began to explain the geography of Cleave, and what efforts had been made to find the missing girl. Her sisters were bewildered by the details. Finally he said, 'I think it would be a good thing if some of you were to come down and satisfy yourselves that everything possible is being done.'

'We should be on our way already,' said Hester, 'had it not been for the calamity of my mother's illness. As it is, Sally and I are both required here to nurse her, and Celia is in a delicate situation. That leaves Betsey—and Corbet. I hardly like to ask . . .'

'Of course I shall accompany her,' said the faithful Colonel Corbet.

'I am returning tomorrow myself,' said Francis, 'and I shall be very glad to take you both along with me, on one condition: Miss Betsey, can you refrain from describing me as a murderer at every posting-house where we stop to change horses?'

Betsey promised, rather sulkily, to behave herself.

Francis left soon afterwards, so deeply preoccupied with his thoughts that he hardly knew where he was going. He had walked all the way down Park Lane and turned into Piccadilly, before he came to his senses and decided to make for his club. At this moment he saw two acquaintances advancing towards him along the pavement. He stopped and was astonished when one of them went straight past him without a word.

'What's the matter with Leyland?' he asked the other man.

'Oh, you must not mind him, my dear Aubrey. People are bound to feel a little awkward, you know. Not being certain whether to offer condolences or congratulations.'

Francis stalked on without another word. His face was grim. Presently he hailed a hackney carriage. He had changed his mind about going to the club. Instead, he gave the address of his lawyer.

## 13

Mr. William Parminter, the Aubreys' family lawyer and man of business, had his chambers in Lincoln's Inn Fields, not far from the house where Caroline Prior lived with the Arthur Reeds—though Francis was not aware of this.

He was shown into a large, sombre room on the ground floor, and Mr. Parminter came forward to meet him.

'I am extremely glad to see you here, my lord. I was on the point of writing to you, as it happens.'

'About that scurrilous story in the *Chronicle*, I collect. Have I any redress?'

'You should have,' said the attorney. He was a big, cheerful man of around fifty. 'Unfortunately these ink-slingers are an artful bunch of scoundrels; they'll probably claim that no one could identify the unnamed characters in their highly coloured fairy-tale—which is nonsense, of course. We shall have to see what can be done. But first of all, my dear sir, do acquaint me with what has been happening at Cleave. Even the public prints usually have some smattering of truth behind their innuendoes.'

Once again Francis recited the bare facts of Ada's dis-appearance. They were easier to explain to Mr. Parminter, who had been to Hoyle Park and thoroughly understood the lie of the land. Presently he fetched an estate map and sat studying it: the deep horseshoe curve of the boundary wall, with the great house set well back from the sea; the fringe of coastline, shaded to denote woodland, and the Wilderness Walk threading its way from one gate to the other, with the cottage marked in, somewhere near the middle.

'It's an intriguing problem,' he said.

'I have only just begun to consider it seriously. Until two hours ago I would have sworn that girl was back in Mount Street; I fully expected to have a pistol held at my head—so many thousand pounds down, and dear Ada may be prevailed upon to break her engagement. Well, I was wrong. Her sisters insist that they don't know where she is, and they are not play-acting, they are grief-stricken and frightened. They honestly believed that I—even Hester believed it, though she ought to know me better.' He laughed, not very happily. 'They are each looking five years older than they pretend, their mother is said to be prostrate, and the house is in a strange state of disarray; I even got a glimpse of old father Gainey, who is generally hidden from view. Rumour has it, in the wine-cellar.'

Mr. Parminter was still frowning over the map with the concentration of a chess-player.

'Your original assumption—that Miss Gainey might have left the estate without being seen—I suppose you were thinking of the Martland gate? Perhaps you do not place much confidence in the solitary witness at the gazebo?'

'Well, that's another stumbling-block; to begin with I decided that she might easily be mistaken, but since then I have spent some time in her company, and I must admit that Miss Caroline Prior is the sort of girl whose evidence cannot be ignored.'

'Caroline Prior? But I know her! That is—if we are speaking of the same person? A younger sister of the lady who . . .'

'Yes.'

'She lives only a few doors from here. What a curious coincidence.'

'I can't see why,' said Francis in his damping way. 'That fellow Reed's a lawyer, is he not? It would be a great deal odder if they didn't live somewhere in this vicinity.'

Mr. Parminter was one of the people who never allowed himself to be intimidated by Lord Francis. He merely laughed, saying, 'She is an intelligent girl. I won't say she is incapable of error, but if there was the remotest uncertainty in her mind I am sure she would be honest and sensible enough to say so.'

'That was exactly my own conclusion.'

'So we have Miss Gainey disappearing in broad daylight, somewhere inside the Hoyle Park boundaries. This is mysterious indeed. What do you know of the visitors who entered the Wilderness that afternoon? Did you not say there were several strangers?'

'A wedding party from Brind Abbas, eminently respectable. Sturdy has taken the trouble to trace them. And then there was the haughty wine merchant . . .'

'Who . . . ?'

'A fellow who drove his wife over from Plymouth in a gig and mortally offended Sam Roebuck at The Ship by refusing to take any refreshment in Cleave. According to his groom, he was a London vintner who turned up his nose at provincial pot-houses.'

'A wine merchant? I think he must be the man who wrote to me. Wait a moment . . .' Mr. Parminter began to burrow through his correspondence.

'He wrote to you?'

'A letter came this morning. Written, I suppose, after the gossip began to spread. Here it is.'

He handed Francis a sheet of paper bearing the ornamental letter-head of Messrs. Baldock and Scroggs, Importers of Fine Wines, with premises at Duke Street, St. James's. The letter was written in a neat, educated hand.

*W. Parminter, Esquire.*
*Dear Sir,*
*Having read an account in the Newspaper of the disappearance of a young lady from the grounds of Hoyle Park, Devonshire on Tuesday last, the nineteenth June, I*

*beg to state that my wife and I were walking in these grounds at about two o'clock on that same afternoon where we saw a person whom we believe to be the young lady in question. She was sitting in the garden of a cottage adjacent to the footpath known as the Wilderness Walk. She was alone and appeared to be in good health. I am afraid this information may not be of much assistance to you, but I felt it was my duty to write.*

*I remain, Sir,*
*Your obedient servant,*
*Gilbert Finch.*

'He sounds damned respectable, too,' said Francis gloomily.

'Well, you can hardly suppose that he was keeping an assignation with Miss Gainey in the presence of his wife.'

'Or that they would have been able to smuggle a fourth person aboard their gig. Alive or dead. And anyway they were too early on the scene. We already knew that they were just behind young Jem Heard, and he reached the village at a quarter past two.'

'Miss Gainey being still in the cottage garden at the half-hour, because Miss Prior saw her there?'

'Yes.' Francis re-read the letter, frowning. 'There's something odd here, Parminter. Why did he write to you?'

'A sense of duty. He could not know that his evidence was superfluous. If it hadn't been for Miss Prior, the Finches would have been the last people to see the girl before she disappeared.'

'Yes, that's true, but it's not what I meant. Why did Finch write to *you*, I wonder? How did he know of your connection with our family? And come to that, why didn't

112

he approach the girl's own parents, they are the people most concerned.'

Parminter stared at him. 'What are you suggesting, sir?'

'Finch read these poisonous insinuations in the *Chronicle*: suppose he had seen something in the wood which might put a different construction on the mystery?'

'Then why did he not say so?'

'Afraid of committing himself on paper—a fear common to all honest men when writing to your learned brethren, my dear Parminter. I'd like to meet the fellow, anyway, and find out what was in his mind. It's too late to go to Duke Street now, they'll have closed for the night. What a confounded nuisance; I'd planned to make an early start in the morning, I'm taking Betsey Gainey and George Corbet with me.'

'Shall I arrange to interview Finch?'

'I'd rather see him myself,' said Francis with his usual bluntness. He then astonished Mr. Parminter by looking a little confused and adding, 'I don't mean to offend you. But I should like to know what Finch has to say before I return to Cleave.'

Who the devil has been trying to teach you manners? wondered Mr. Parminter. Aloud, he said: 'If you would care to dine with me I could send my clerk along to Baldock and Scroggs, just in case there is any hope of getting hold of Mr. Finch tonight.'

Francis agreed to both these propositions, the clerk was despatched on his errand, and presently the two men went upstairs to dine in a faint areole of candle-light, while the brightness of a long June day still poured in through the tall windows.

Presently Mr. Parminter's clerk came back from Duke Street; there had been a nightwatchman on duty at Baldock and Scroggs, who had been persuaded to consult a list of addresses. Gilbert Finch, a junior employee, had lodgings in Kentish Town at the house of a Mr. Walters.

Francis set off once more in a hackney carriage, northwards through real London and across the New Road into the growing suburbs that spread over the green fields of Highbury and Islington. Some of the houses seemed to have sprung up ill-advisedly on any odd piece of ground, but there were also prettily planned groups of terraces and squares which were rather misleadingly known as 'Towns': Camden, Canning, Kentish and so forth. Francis surveyed the rows of brick and stucco with an appraising eye and did sums in his head. There was a good deal of money to be made out of this type of speculation.

Number Six, Pine Apple Place, was a modest villa in a pleasant district. Francis got out of the carriage and told the coachman to wait. The window on the right of the front door presented a golden rectangle of lamplight, with two figures lit up, as though in a peepshow: a pretty, dark girl in a pink dress sat close to the lamp, sewing, and smiling at something a large young man was apparently reading aloud to her from a book in his hand. Seen remotely through the glass and the gauzy nimbus of a net curtain, this little domestic interior had a curious charm.

The front door was opened by a schoolboy, obviously the son of the house. Francis asked for Mr. Finch.

A woman's voice, from somewhere upstairs, called out: 'Who is it, Tom?'

'A gentleman wanting Mr. Finch, Ma.'

The large young man from the peepshow looked out into the hall.

'Someone for me, Tom? Oh . . . ?' He stopped, uncertain.

'Mr. Finch? I am Lord Francis Aubrey, and I am most anxious to have a word in private with you.'

'Oh. I had not expected—anything I can do to assist your lordship—but it is not very—that is to say . . .'

Gilbert Finch, who looked a tolerably sensible young man, stood stammering in his doorway in a feeble and irresolute manner. Francis knew that the unexpected disclosure of his title was apt to have this effect, and he found it extremely irritating. His natural arrogance was due entirely to a sense of his own ability, but he was not a snob, and he could have done without the reverence for rank which made so many people stupider than they were already.

'I hope I am not putting you to any inconvenience,' he said insincerely, advancing on Mr. Finch who was obliged to get out of his way.

Francis looked beyond him into the small, cheerful, not very tidy parlour. There was a table with a cloth laid for a meal at one end, and at the other a stack of books, and several magazines. There were a good many china ornaments, as well as a half-trimmed bonnet on a stand, and a linnet in a birdcage. The girl in pink was trying to retire unobtrusively, which was difficult, as there was only one door, and they were in danger of colliding as he came in. He made her a slight bow.

'My wife, sir,' said Finch.

'Please do not go away on my account, Mrs. Finch. In fact I would prefer you to remain, if you have no objection, for you were also at Hoyle Park on the nineteenth, were you not?'

'Yes, my lord,' she said in a low voice, curtseying and gazing at the floor.

As soon as they were all seated, Francis turned to Finch

saying, 'You wrote to Mr. Parminter of Lincoln's Inn. May I ask why?'

'I thought—in view of the circumstances—we had been in the grounds of Hoyle Park that afternoon, and I thought we ought to give an account of ourselves. Even though we had nothing useful to relate.'

'I appreciate your public spirit. But what made you choose Mr. Parminter as your correspondent?'

'I heard he was Lord Eltham's attorney. In my place of business, my lord, there are always gentlemen talking, one cannot help overhearing such scraps of information.'

'Yes, I see. It did not strike you that the persons most anxious for details of Miss Gainey's disappearance must be her own relations? She has a great many of them, here in London. You did not think of approaching them?'

Gilbert Finch shook his head. He seemed to have some difficulty in finding anything to say.

'I can tell you why my husband wrote to Mr. Parminter.'

'Can you, Mrs. Finch?'

She had recovered from her shyness and was regarding him steadily with a pair of large brown eyes. 'I thought he must be a more respectable person than those Gaineys. I know one should not cast stones, and I'm sorry for that young woman if something horrid has happened to her, but she did bring it on herself, and they say she has a lot of dreadfully vulgar sisters who are no better than they should be. Of course there are people who don't care, who have no reputation to lose—but Gilbert has his position to think of. He can't associate with loose women.'

Gilbert was by now as red as a turkey-cock. 'I wish you'd learn to hold your tongue!'

'Oh. Have I said something I shouldn't?'

'Certainly not,' said Francis, catching Gilbert's eye with

a gleam of man-to-man commiseration. 'But I must own that I am disappointed.'

'How is that, my lord?' asked Finch, beginning to regain his composure.

'You have read the story in the newspaper. I am sure you know that I am the person alluded to in those veiled accusations. When I found you had written to my attorney, I was seized with the idea that you might have some evidence to support my innocence. But I assume that this is not so?'

'No, I am afraid not, sir. We have unwillingly misled you.'

'It can't be helped. I suppose you saw nothing suspicious while you were in the wood?'

There had been nothing, they admitted regretfully. They had been returning from Plymouth, Gilbert said, where he had been engaged on some business for his employers, and he had got permission to combine this trip with a short holiday; there were so many interesting places to visit on the way. The Wilderness Walk had quite lived up to their expectations. They had sauntered along in a state of romantic wonder, admiring the fine prospects at every turn of the footpath, and presently they had come on the cottage, with Ada Gainey sitting in the garden in her white muslin dress.

'What was she doing? Did she speak to you?'

'No, sir. And she was not doing anything precisely, just sitting on a chair. We thought—we didn't know who she was then, of course—and we both thought she looked a very interesting young woman, didn't we, my love?'

'I thought she was a hussy,' replied his love darkly.

Finch shot an apprehensive glance at her, and Francis was amused. He had decided that the young wine merchant, though dotingly in love with his pretty wife, had not yet learnt to manage her.

Sticking to the matter in hand, he asked: 'Did you meet anyone else in the wood?'

'There was a man, a villager, carrying something like a bag of tools; we did not meet him, because he was going in the same direction. He was some way ahead of us and visible nearly all the time through the trees.'

This, of course, was Jem Heard, the carpenter.

'He spoke to Miss Gainey,' remarked the girl. 'You remember, Gilbert?'

'Yes, you are right. He did.'

Francis had been feeling that all these questions were a waste of time. He became suddenly alert. 'Are you absolutely certain of that? You could not be mistaken?'

'No, there was not the smallest doubt,' they replied, more or less in unison, both slightly baffled by his sharpened curiosity. 'Is it important?'

'It might be. Because Heard swore that he never spoke to Miss Gainey, nor she to him. Were you able to hear what was said?'

'No, we were too far behind. We just caught the sound of voices,' said Finch, 'and he stopped for a minute or so, and then went on. They could not have exchanged more than a couple of sentences.'

'I thought he was bringing her a message. I said so all along, didn't I, Gilbert?'

'Lord Francis does not want to know what you said all along, my dear,' Finch told her repressively.

'Well, he might, if that was the villain who abducted Miss Gainey.'

'No, he cannot have been the abductor,' said Francis. 'He spent the rest of the afternoon at the sawmill, in the company of three witnesses. But that small item of new knowledge is odd enough to need explaining; it may lead somewhere in the end. I am grateful to you.'

When he rose to go, Finch came out to the carriage with him.

'I hope you won't put too much weight on my wife's opinion,' he said diffidently. 'About that fellow delivering a message—she had nothing whatever to go on. I should not like him to be unjustly suspected.'

'Mrs. Finch is given to reading novels, perhaps?'

'Well, you see, my lord, she is very young. She does not understand what harm she might do.'

'But this short conversation between Miss Gainey and Heard did actually take place? That was not an invention?'

'That was no invention,' said Gilbert Finch.

# 14

Lavinia and Caroline had been bickering at intervals, ever since the morning that Caroline had vanished into the Wilderness and reappeared from the seashore in the company of Lord Francis.

'I don't know how you could be so inconsiderate! And after I'd expressly asked you not to go inside the wood. You broke your promise . . .'

'Well, I know I did, and I've said I'm sorry; can't we take the rest for granted?'

It was Tuesday, four days after the ludicrous adventure of the smugglers' passage, and Caroline was getting very tired of her sister's reproaches, but Lavinia seemed to be rather enjoying her sense of ill-usage.

'When Duffet drove up in the gig without you, and when he told me that he'd asked everywhere, and Mrs. Harper had seen you enter the wood—I thought my heart would have stopped beating altogether. I made him drive me round to the village, no one knew what to do for the best, we began to fear you must have suffered the same fate as that other poor girl—and when you came stumping up from the harbour, your dress all mussed up with sea-weed and your hair like a haystack, and with that man beside you—I could have died of mortification!'

'You should have been glad to discover that I hadn't suffered the fate of that other poor girl—especially as we still don't know what it was. As for Lord Francis, he probably saved me from drowning, and you were not at all civil to him.'

'He was not at all civil to me. He put that wet basket on my feet, and I am persuaded he did it on purpose.'

'Yes, I dare say he did. He seems to have a very odd sense of humour. For heaven's sake, Lavinia, let us stop wrangling. Shall we go for a walk? It will do us both good.'

But Lavinia did not want to go out, she was sure it would rain. The weather had broken on Sunday; it was now grey and cheerless and there was no question of sea-bathing.

'Then I'll go by myself,' said Caroline.

'No, Caro! I absolutely forbid you—I shan't have a moment's peace. Why must you be so restless?'

'Well, I've got nothing to read, for one thing.'

'That's hardly my fault,' said Lavinia in a martyred accent. 'I didn't drop the library books in the sea.'

Caroline went upstairs to her bedroom; she was afraid of losing her temper.

On the landing she met her niece Vinny.

'Oh, Aunt Caro, will you come and help me with my paper dolls?'

'Not just now, my dear. Why don't you go downstairs and ask your Mama?'

Let Lavinia take the trouble to amuse her brats for a change, she thought, in the blessed solitude of her own room. I'm sick of acting as an unpaid nursemaid. And I'm sick of pandering to her timidity, calming her fears, protecting her from Arthur's displeasure when she irritates him, listening in a respectful silence when Arthur wants to play Socrates. He is a good man, and I suppose a capable man, but he is too pompous ever to say anything interesting. And Lavinia is too stupid to have anything interesting to say.

At this point she became suddenly horrified by the train of her thoughts. She had never felt like this before. She was really very fond of all the Reeds (and no one was perfect, after all). Only something had happened to her that morning on the beach; it must be the result of listening to Lord Francis. He was rather a disturbing person, and he had made her feel discontented.

She went to the window and looked out. The hillside was desolate, the trees in the Wilderness tossed their branches in the wind, and all the greens of summer now seemed listless and drear . . . She could hear the waves crashing on the rocks at the foot of the combe.

It was exactly a week since the hot afternoon when Ada Gainey disappeared. Surely she must be dead by now? In some illogical way, the bad weather seemed to make it more certain. As though she might have been living a secret life of Rousseau-like simplicity in the woods until it got too cold—which was absurd. Sooner or later her dead body must come to light; only some extraordinary freak of circumstance could have concealed it until now. Perhaps she really had been carried out to sea. Caroline imagined her white face staring blindly up from one of the rock pools, with her hair floating round her. She shivered.

It was as though Ada's ghost already haunted the combe. The lovely, timeless, uncomplicated world of Caroline's childhood was lost for ever. Day after golden day of beach and bracken, in which nothing had ever happened.

Although, to be honest, a good deal had happened during their last visit. Lavinia had got engaged to Lord Francis, the engagement had been broken, their father had lost all his money . . . Caroline sat on her bed, and tried to call up the past. The disappointment of hearing that Lavinia was going to marry that dull little man. How strange, surely the Lord Francis of those days was much less positive than the person he had since become? The abrupt manner had been there, but she could not remember him saying anything interesting. She could not actually remember him saying anything at all. Because of the engagement the Priors had been continually invited up to Hoyle Park, an interruption to their summer pursuits which had annoyed Caroline very much. She recalled the schoolroom there, Jack Eltham boasting about his horse, and his three sisters, the Ladies Maria, Lucy and Anne, in white dresses with black spencers and black stockings . . . What else? Waking in the middle of the night to hear Lavinia sobbing her heart out, choking and gasping in a most alarming manner. Unable to make her stop, Caroline had eventually got up and gone to fetch Mama. More crying and whispering, and the next morning Lavinia stayed in bed, and Miss Mason told Caroline that her sister's ruined hopes should be a warning to her. 'It is a mistake to accept a proposal of marriage on too short an acquaintance.' And it was that very day the fatal letter arrived from London, and she could still remember her mother's face growing paler as she read, and the odd note in her voice: 'I am afraid they are in some kind of difficulty at the bank.'

Yes, but wait a moment. There was something curious about these recollections. Caroline went through them again in her mind, as though she was sorting and arranging a hand at cards, but the result was still the same. She went downstairs into their private parlour, where Lavinia was writing to Arthur. (She had apparently got rid of Vinny and the paper dolls.)

'I want to ask you something,' said Caroline, coming straight to the point. 'Why did you break off your engagement to Francis Aubrey?'

Lavinia looked up. 'You know very well why—because Papa had lost all his money. And one is expected to offer a man his freedom under those circumstances.' She sounded glib.

'While the man—if he is a gentleman—is expected to decline the offer and stand by his commitments. Apparently Lord Francis wouldn't, as it has been held against him ever since.'

Lavinia said nothing.

'Only that's not what really happened. Is it?' said Caroline.

'I don't know what you mean.'

'Your engagement was already broken when Mama got the letter about the bank failing. I knew that at the time, of course, but I was so overwhelmed—seeing Mama and Papa in such a state of misery and indecision; the distress of having to leave Curzon Street, all our things being sold

—and your not getting married seemed to be all part of the general disaster. But it cannot have been so. What was the true reason?'

'We did not suit,' said Lavinia in a low voice. 'I could never have returned his affection.'

An image slid into Caroline's consciousness of the younger and surprisingly silent Francis gazing at Lavinia with a kind of throttled desperation. Good God, she thought, he was hopelessly in love with her. It wasn't the money after all.

'Do you not think,' she said, 'that the situation ought to have been made plain? In justice to him.'

'No, I don't,' retorted Lavinia in a flurry of agitation. 'He deserved nothing better, considering the brutal way he behaved, and anyway, I dared not tell Mama . . .'

She gave a little gasp of fright. What had she not dared to tell Mama? Had the infatuated Francis terrified her by trying to awaken some response to his own passion? Caroline was old enough to recognise that he had the power of attracting women, in spite of his unromantic appearance, but she doubted whether Lavinia, at eighteen, was able to sense this attraction. To her, Francis was probably a frog-prince visible only as a frog.

'I dare say he did not mean to be a brute.'

'Of course he did. He nearly killed poor Alfred.'

Who in the world was Alfred? Another figure emerged dimly from the past: a young ensign of militia, whose mother had rented one of the houses in Belvedere Terrace, Alfred Pyke or Dyke or something of the sort, tall and slim, with wind-blown locks and the profile of a demi-god.

'Lavinia! Do you mean to say you had two men fighting over you?'

Lavinia dissolved into tears. 'You mustn't tell anyone!

You mustn't tell Arthur! I should die of shame. Caro, promise you won't tell Arthur.'

'My dearest Vin, of course I won't tell a soul. Though perhaps, having gone so far, you would feel easier if you told me.'

Lavinia mopped her eyes dolefully, and said she supposed Caroline would blame her for everything. 'I was wrong to accept Francis, I admit that. I think I was too much surprised and gratified by his asking me, because the Aubreys are so very grand. We had nothing in common. I could not understand the half of what he was saying, sometimes he sounded cross and it would turn out he was joking, and at other times—well, he was far too clever for me, besides being too old.'

'Old? But even now he cannot be more than . . .' Caroline stopped. Luckily Lavinia was too preoccupied to notice her confusion.

'He was close on thirty and not at all handsome. So different from Alfred, who was the kind of lover every girl dreams of. I lost my heart to Alfred at the first glance. Yet what could we do? He was quite ineligible, hadn't a penny besides his pay. Imagine telling Mama that I wanted to jilt Lord Francis Aubrey and follow the drum!'

'Did no one guess?'

'No. It was all over in about a week. We went on a picnic to Brind, to explore the abbey ruins: Francis and Alfred and I and about a dozen others, and there was a married woman to act as chaperone, only she wasn't very particular how we behaved, and presently Alfred and I contrived to escape from the rest. We wandered off into those meadows, down by the river.' Lavinia's narrative had slowed down, she sat twisting the fringe of the tablecloth between her nervous fingers. 'I was eighteen, I did not appreciate the folly—years later I met a woman whose husband had served in the same regiment as Alfred, and she said he had a very bad reputation. We sat on the grass and he—flirted with me in a dreadfully improper way. And then, all of a sudden, there was Francis in front of us, and his face—I can't describe it—he was like a man possessed.

'We both jumped to our feet. He seized Alfred by the throat and nearly strangled him. Alfred managed to force his hands apart, so that he could breathe, and then Francis knocked him down. I don't know how he was able to, he must be very strong. And after that he picked up a stick that was lying near, and he hit Alfred with it, over and over again. It was horrible. By the time he'd finished, poor Alfred was hunched up on the ground and groaning, but Francis wouldn't let me do anything to help him. He dragged me off to his curricle and drove me straight back here to the farm. I tried to pretend there was nothing wrong—we had the groom perched up behind us—but Francis never spoke to me once in six miles.

'When we arrived, he brought me as far as the door. He said no one knew what I had been doing, they thought I had come home with a headache, and Alfred would not dare to tell tales. So he would allow me to break off the engagement, because in that way I should not lose my character. Then he drove off and left me. And can you wonder,' added Lavinia, 'that I never wanted to come down here or meet him again?'

'No, indeed. Poor Vin, it was a wretched business for you altogether. But what did you tell Mama?'

'I let her think we had simply had a lovers' quarrel, I had no choice. She was sure we would make it up, and when the bank failed she expected this would bring him hurrying to my side. She kept hoping to hear from him, while I was half hoping to hear from Alfred. Needless to say, I never had a word from either.'

'You must have been very unhappy.'

'We all were. It was a horrid time, wasn't it? At least I was spared a lot of awkward questions, that was one blessing.'

'Not such a blessing for Lord Francis, perhaps.'

Lavinia shifted uncomfortably. 'I didn't go round telling people he had deserted me. If they jumped to that conclusion, how was I to stop them? You wouldn't have had me make a public confession?'

'No, of course not. All the same, I cannot help wishing that things had not turned out so awkwardly. Did you know that the broken engagement is still a subject for malicious gossip? I heard it mentioned the other morning at Miss Weatherby's, as an indication that Francis Aubrey is a man who might rob his own nephew, and then perhaps commit murder to avoid discovery.'

'Well, I am sorry,' said Lavinia, with a rather tremulous touch of defiance, 'but for all we know, he may have killed the girl. It seems as though she must have been killed, and he had a reason to get rid of her, quite apart from the money. He cannot have wanted Eltham to marry such a person, and if once he lost his temper—I've seen him in a rage, Caro. You haven't.'

Mrs. Harper had said something very like this, and there were no doubt plenty of other people who felt the same. Caroline saw Francis as a prisoner in a cage of prejudice. If only he were to come back from London with a solution to the mystery. Unfortunately she did not think this was at all likely. She was convinced that Ada had never left Cleave.

## 15

'I wish you would try to be a little less despondent, Jack,' said Anne Dangerfield to her brother.

He gave her the reproachful glance of a hurt child, and returned to his brooding contemplation of the view. They were in the orangery, a glass-fronted pavilion attached to the south wall of the great house; it was a pleasant place to sit on a windy day. In front of them lay a sweep of lawn, an invisible ha-ha, a further green expanse of open parkland, and then, along the coastline, the dark smudge of the Wilderness that beautiful wood which its owner had come to look on with horror and loathing.

'You'll do yourself no good by moping,' persisted Lady Anne. She was a fair, plump, good-natured girl of nine-teen; her husband, a tall and rakishly handsome young man was talking to Octavius Barrow.

'What is the good of pretending to be sanguine,' protested Jack, 'when every hour that passes must confirm our worst fears? My poor girl—why did I ever leave her? She hated this place. At first I thought she was merely indulging a Londoner's dislike of the country, but now I am beginning to think she must have had a premonition of disaster.'

Anne could think of no answer to this, or at least none that Jack would find acceptable. He got up and began pacing about the orangery, sometimes stopping to stare at some exotic plant, though probably without the faintest idea what he was doing.

'He is much worse,' said Anne, in a low voice to her companions, 'since he read that piece in the newspaper.

Why so many of our acquaintance felt obliged to send us cuttings from the *St. James's Chronicle* . . .'

'Do you think he believes those hints about your uncle?' asked Octavius uneasily.

'Yes,' said Philip Dangerfield.

At the same moment Anne said, 'No. Well, I don't think he knows what to believe. I must own I am rather dreading Uncle Francis's return from London.'

'And in the meantime,' said her husband, 'you have invited two strange females to drink tea with us. As if we haven't troubles enough already.'

'I thought it would do Jack good if he had to subdue his feelings a little,' Anne sounded defensive. 'He has met Miss Prior, I think he admires her. And they are old family friends. You have seen them Tavy—the ladies who are staying at Martland Farm. What are they like?'

'Mrs. Reed is about thirty years old, beautiful but insipid. Miss Caroline is nothing out of the common; she has a brown complexion and her nose is too long.'

'Heaven preserve us!' Philip closed his eyes.

'Oh, Tavy! You are so critical. I quite long to see them again.'

'But my dear Lady Anne, do you think they will come?'

'I hope so. I sent the carriage to fetch them.'

A few minutes later the butler conducted Miss Caroline Prior into the orangery, alone.

She made her sister's apologies with a well-bred facility, saying that she had a headache, brought on by the cold wind. (In fact, Lavinia did not want to meet any of the Aubreys, and she had not much wanted Caroline to go to the Hall without her, but it would have been difficult for them both to refuse, when the carriage was standing at the door.)

Lord Eltham came forward to shake hands with her, and Caroline thought he looked dreadful; about ten years older in a matter of days. He also looked surprised, and it dawned on her that he did not know she had been invited, and must think her intrusive and impertinent to call on his sister at such a time.

She found herself sitting on an iron garden chair beside Lady Anne, making conversation. She did not like to ask if there was any fresh news, and apparently Lord Francis had not yet returned from London. She wished she had not come.

It was nearly eight o'clock, and after another grey day the sun had come out in a tantalising way, and a calm, paradisal glow hung over the evening. Some liveried footmen put up a table among the palm trees and brought out a silver tea-tray.

Presently they heard the sound of a carriage coming along the drive.

'I wonder who that is,' said Anne.

Philip stepped out of the orangery on to the grass, to investigate.

'It's your uncle,' he reported. 'And there are some people with him—Hester Gainey, by Jove! No, it's not Hester —devilish like her, though. Why, it must be Ada!'

'Ada!' exclaimed Jack. His tea-cup splintered on the stone flags, as he jumped up and ran out of the orangery to join his brother-in-law. Then he came to a sudden stop.

'But that isn't Ada, there isn't the least resemblance— that's only Betsey. You fool, Philip. Why did you have to raise my hopes?'

Lord Francis had now come round the corner of the house, accompanied by a dark man who had an air of military competence and a handsome, showy young woman with a voluptuous figure and a magnificent head of hair, the colour of a copper warming-pan.

So that was what they meant by a Golden Gainey, thought Caroline. Ada had not been at all like her sisters.

'Oh, my dear Eltham,' exclaimed Betsey, 'I hear there is still no news.'

He took her hand without speaking.

They all trooped into the orangery, and Caroline noticed that although Eltham greeted the military-looking man, whose name was Corbet, he appeared not to notice his uncle. The only time she had seen them together, they were quarrelling, and she did not suppose the strain of the last week had improved matters. Or perhaps they were simply preoccupied by the awkwardness of the introduction that had to be made.

It would have been impossible, in ordinary circumstances, for Lady Anne Dangerfield and Miss Betsey Gainey ever to meet, though they might observe each other stonily in Hyde Park or at the Opera, and share the same choice of friends and lovers. Colonel Corbet was apologising in an undertone to Mr. Dangerfield for putting his wife in such an uncomfortable fix.

'Think nothing of it, my dear fellow. The main thing is to get this business cleared up before we have poor Eltham in a strait-jacket.'

In fact the peer's sister and the courtesan were both so high up on their own particular trees that they were able to talk to each other quite unaffectedly, Anne full of sympathy for Betsey's anxiety. Fresh tea-cups were sent for (the travellers had already dined) and Caroline began to feel more than ever that she was an intruder at this curious family conclave. She ought to leave, but it was difficult; she had given Lavinia her solemn word that she would not attempt to walk home alone. Perhaps she could get hold of Octavius, the other outsider, and ask him to escort her? At the moment, however, Octavius was taken up with watching and listening and enjoying the piquancy of the situation.

'Good evening, Miss Prior. What are you doing here?' asked Lord Francis, with his usual want of tact.

'I was invited to drink tea, sir, but I feel I am very much in the way.'

She was almost angling for one of his barbed retorts, and was disconcerted when he said, 'You could never be in the way, as far as I am concerned. Besides which, I owe you an apology. I believe you were right all along: that unfortunate girl never left the estate.'

'If that is so,' said Caroline slowly, 'I assure you that I can take no pleasure in such a petty triumph. I wish with all my heart that you had found her alive and well in London.'

Lady Anne began to ask him about a scurrilous paragraph in one of the newspapers.

'Oh, has that already arrived in Devonshire?'

'We had half a dozen copies by this morning's mail.'

'What puzzles me,' said Philip Dangerfield, 'is how the affair got into print so quickly.'

'That is the strangest part of the whole business,' said Francis. 'An account sent through the ordinary mail could hardly have reached London in time to appear in Friday's *Chronicle*. I was a good deal mystified until I remembered that Jack wrote to Hester, the day after Ada disappeared, and sent his letter by special post delivery, from door to door. If the postboy had been bribed to take a second letter to London with him, it could have reached the *Chronicle* in time. In fact, I think an enquiry at the Brind Abbas post office might lead to some interesting disclosures. I must say, I should like to know who it was did me such a bad turn. I wonder if Jack remembers which of the men took his letter up to Brind.'

He turned to his nephew, but Jack was talking earnestly to Betsey. Both the Dangerfields and Octavius chimed in with a chorus of questions, and Anne succeeded in distracting her uncle by asking him if he had accomplished anything useful in London.

'I suppose you saw Parminter?'

'Yes, and I also saw the haughty wine merchant, a perfectly harmless young man who lives in Kentish Town. He and his wife told me of one very small circumstance that is worth repeating; they came through the Wilderness a little way behind Jem Heard—we knew that already, of course—and they both insist that Jem stopped at the cottage and had a short conversation with Ada. Yet Jem himself, when we asked him that evening, denied ever speaking to her. Isn't that so, Octavius? You were there.'

'Yes, sir. He did. That's very odd.'

'But surely you don't imagine Jem would have stood a chance . . .' Philip broke off, constrained by the presence of Betsey.

'No, I don't think that,' said Francis. 'But anything out of the ordinary may be important, where we have so little to go on.'

Jack had been describing to the newcomers all the unsuccessful efforts that had been made to find some trace of Ada, including a minute search of the great house itself.

'Good God!' said Francis to Anne. 'Is that what he's been doing while I was away? Was it really necessary? I suppose all the servants have given notice.'

She shook her head and glanced apprehensively at her

brother, but he was still talking to Corbet and Betsey.

'Now,' he said unhappily, 'we are reduced to digging in the wood. Anywhere that the soil seems to have been disturbed.'

'Digging?' repeated Betsey. 'That is horrible!'

'Have you no idea who is responsible?' asked Colonel Corbet. 'I suppose it must be one of your own people, inside this closed circle. Lord Francis was telling us, on the way down, that they are all men of excellent character, so the most likely explanation is a sudden onset of madness—I have known of such cases in the army—but there are generally quite a number of warning signs; surely there must be someone you suspect?'

It seemed to Caroline as though everyone in the orangery was waiting for Jack's reply.

And just then a solemn procession was seen approaching across the grass. The head gardener, carefully carrying something small that was wrapped in sacking, and followed by two other men armed with spades. All three wore their working clothes, with mud thick on their boots.

Jack got up and moved stiffly, like a sleepwalker, towards the glass door. The rest of the party crowded after him. No one spoke.

The head gardener held up his trophy. 'I think your lordship ought to see what Smith uncovered on a patch of ground about a hundred yards east of the cottage.'

He lifted a piece of sacking, and revealed two small, rather dirty white objects that Caroline at first mistook for the dead bodies of two doves. Then she realised they were looking at a pair of white kid slippers, soaking wet and stained with red Devon soil.

'No!' whispered Jack. It was almost a sob. He reached out and stroked the soft leather with his fingers.

134

Betsey said: 'Those are Ada's shoes. I helped her choose them, before she came away. So it's true. She's dead—my little sister.' She broke into a storm of weeping.

Francis was questioning the gardener. 'How were the shoes buried, exactly?'

'They were only a few inches below the surface, my lord. Scrabbled into a pocket of leaf-mould. What we thought . . .' He indicated his two subordinates. 'It was like as though someone might have filled in a grave, and then found the shoes had been left behind. We shan't find the grave this evening, my lord, it's getting too dark in the wood. We'll start looking again at first light.'

'Yes. That must be done, of course,' said Francis. He spoke to his nephew, putting a hand on his arm. 'Jack, my dear boy, I'm afraid this has been a great shock to you . . .'

Jack swung round on him. 'Don't touch me, you damned hypocrite!'

Francis stepped back as though he had been struck.

'Why did you do it?' demanded Jack. 'Did you think I cared so much about the money? I've guessed for years that you were swindling the estate, I could have turned a blind eye to that. Why did you have to kill her?'

Francis did not answer. He took another step backwards, and was brought up against the tendrils of the great vine that clambered up the orangery wall to the roof. Beneath it he stood, a small and lonely figure, completely at a loss, as he glanced swiftly at each of the surrounding faces and then back to Eltham. His expression was bewildered and incredulous; the expression of a man who was used to being misunderstood by the common herd (and perhaps even enjoyed it) but had never in his life expected to be accused of two especially mean and hateful crimes by a member of his own family.

That was how it seemed to Caroline. She found she was trembling with anger and compassion. All the pity she should have felt for Ada was suddenly directed towards Francis. She wanted to go to him, to break through that cold ring of isolation, and what held her back was not the fear of what the others might think, it was the fear that he himself might reject her. She hesitated, trying to pluck up her courage, and then she found she had lost her chance. A servant arrived to say the carriage was waiting to take her home. It was a moment of sheer anti-climax.

Anne was helping Colonel Corbet to calm the half hysterical Betsey; she had sent for her maid and her vinaigrette. She looked up, abstractedly.

'Oh, Miss Prior! I am sorry you have had such a disagreeable evening. And I don't like your going all alone in the carriage—Tavy! You'll drive round to Martland with Miss Prior, won't you? Briggs will take you back to the Rectory afterwards.'

So there was no help for it, she was handed into the chaise, Octavius got in beside her, and they set off on the journey that would take them round practically four sides of a square: along the carriage drive, up the hill from the village, back by the main road and down into Martland. It was a clear evening, less than a week after the longest day, so that although the ground was deep in shadow (too dark, under the trees, to reveal that lonely grave) the sky was pale and luminous. They set out in silence; there was plenty to think about.

'They'll never charge him!' said Octavius presently.

'I should hope not. There is no evidence against him. Lord Eltham was too distressed to know what he was saying.'

'In any case they would never touch a man of his rank.

Or would they, do you think? How is one to know?'

He seemed to be very anxious on this point, it was more than just his usual curiosity, and Caroline, studying him in the light that came through the carriage windows, was rather startled by what she saw. He was very white and he seemed unable to stop fidgeting; his hands worked up and down, plucking at his coat-buttons, his cravat, his fob. Was this all due to the ghastly possibility of the girl's body lying buried in the wood? Some people could not bear the sight of blood. Of course there had not been any blood, so far, but those draggled shoes were enough to set a lively imagination racing.

She decided that it would be better for them both to talk about something quite trivial, and asked him, more or less at random, if he would deliver a message to Mrs. Harper.

'Oh, very well. If you wish. That is—I may not see her again for some time. I may have to go away almost immediately. Perhaps tomorrow.'

She was astonished. Earlier that evening she had heard him persuading Philip Dangerfield to go out for a day's sea-fishing.

'Are you off to Bodmin?' she asked, knowing that one of his brothers was a curate there.

'Bodmin? Certainly not. It's no concern of—I am not accountable to my family, you know.'

A few seconds later he said, 'I am sick of Oxford. If the war was not over, I'd join the army.'

She did not know what to make of these jerky pronouncements.

They were now driving down into Martland Combe. The carriage drew up outside the farm, and Caroline got out, saying good night to Octavius.

Her mind was weighed down with all the painful memories of the evening, she was still re-living the scene in the orangery—but as soon as she went indoors she found herself faced with a new and quite unexpected situation.

Arthur had arrived at the farm while she was out. Horrified by the rumours of what was happening at Hoyle Park, he had come to take his family back to London. They were to spend the rest of the summer at Ramsgate.

## *16*

It was no good saying she did not want to leave Devonshire. No one would understand or care. Lavinia had never wanted to come back to Martland, Nurse hated the place, and although the children had enjoyed the first week, the restrictions following Ada's disappearance had irked them, and the weather had been a disappointment.

So Caroline accepted Arthur's decree without comment, went to bed raging against the helplessness of women, and lay awake thinking about Francis Aubrey. She was very unhappy, for two reasons; because she feared he might soon be arrested for murder, and because she never expected to see him again—two disasters which at the moment seemed to her about equally serious, though she had to admit that he was hardly likely to agree. She could even imagine how the comparison would entertain him. How curious it was, this forging of a bond of sympathy out of the unlikely metal of that gift for irony. She now thought Francis more interesting, more unusual, than anyone else she knew. Having been charmed by his lively and original mind, she was bound to recognise the physical expressions of that liveliness: the quick light of appreciation in those very acute grey eyes, the subtle inflexions of his voice, the assured and decisive movements. It was impossible to believe that she had ever considered him dull or ugly, and she was now convinced that he had not done any of the things he was suspected of, though she would have found it difficult to explain why.

She lay stiff with misery, staring upwards into the void of darkness. Her window rattled in its frame, as the wind sighed through the funnel of the combe.

She began to think about Octavius. Arthur's arrival had diverted her attention, but it was a fact that Octavius had behaved very oddly in the carriage—so oddly, indeed, that she was convinced somebody at Hoyle Park ought to hear about it. But who? Eltham was in her bad books; she was sorry for him, but he seemed to be entirely ruled by sensibility and prejudice, and she did not feel quite at home with either of the Dangerfields. There was Francis himself, surely he had more right than anyone to be told of the possibility of something new in the way of evidence.

She slept at last, uneasily, and woke early. Still feeling tired, she got up to do her packing with a curious sense of unreality. The post-chaises would not arrive until eleven. (They had to have two of them this time, to convey such a large party, and Arthur was grumbling about the expense.) Caroline got hold of the youngest Duffet boy and bribed him to go up to the great house and deliver a note to Lord Francis.

Then she went and sat on a bench outside the farmhouse. The weather had cleared, the sun was shining steadily out of a fathomless blue sky; it would have been a splendid morning for the beach. She could hear Lavinia and Nurse, through an upstairs window; they were getting the younger children ready for the journey. Arthur was in the yard, fussing about the baggage. Vinny and Ben were giving each other a last ride on the swing, and chanting a nursery rhyme which had stuck in their heads the last few days, because it seemed to be in some mysterious way appropriate:

> 'The man in the wilderness said to me,
> "How many strawberries grow in the sea?"
> I answered him as I thought good,
> "As many red herrings as grow in the wood." '

And who was the man in the Wilderness, that shadowy figure who must exist in some guise or other, behind the disappearance of Ada Gainey?

High up on the hillside the wicket-gate opened in the long stone wall. The morning was so quiet that she could hear the hinges creak, right down here in the valley. She saw Francis Aubrey coming down the little track that led through the gorse and bracken.

'Good morning, Miss Prior,' he was saying a few minutes later. 'I came as fast as I could.'

'I hope I haven't brought you here for nothing,' said Caroline with a sudden loss of confidence.

'Well, even if you have, I shan't complain. It seemed quite an event this morning that anyone should actually seek my company. I was beginning to feel like a leper.'

He spoke lightly, but there was a hint of real pain in his voice. His eyes were wary, and she did not think he had slept much either.

'I'm sure they cannot all be against you!' she said. 'Surely Mr. Dangerfield and Lady Anne . . .'

'Suspicion is very contagious, you know. Betsey said some extremely bitter things last night, after you left. One can hardly blame her, poor creature—she had to vent her fears on somebody—but the effect was not pleasant. Now old Mansard is down here, full of magisterial zeal, with his godson, Charles Richmond, whom he has sworn in as a special constable. I understand that Richmond is to have the embarrassing duty of conveying me to the county gaol.'

'But that is outrageous! Do you mean—have they found the grave?'

'Not yet. That's why I am still at large. They are all hard at it in the wood, with Mansard giving advice. He's a great one for digging out his foxes.' He caught her expression of distaste. 'Now I have shocked you.'

'Why do you always have to talk like that?' she demanded, angrily. 'Can't you see how much harm it does? Can you wonder that people are hostile when they hear you saying things that sound so callous?'

Francis's normally clear skin had turned a dark, plum red. He was apparently lost for words.

'I beg your pardon,' said Caroline (though she could not think why she was apologising: it was about time someone told him a few home truths). 'To come to the point, sir, has it ever struck you that Octavius Barrow might have had a hand in the mystery?'

'That young rattle?'

'He is threatening to leave home without telling anyone where he is going.'

She repeated everything Octavius had said last night in the carriage, and described his undoubted state of agitation. Francis was soon listening with the greatest concentration.

'Octavius? I wonder. That would at least explain the curious answer I got from Jem Heard.'

'The carpenter? Have you seen him, then?'

'Yes, an hour ago. I told him there were two witnesses who claimed he was talking to Miss Gainey shortly before she vanished. He replied that he had quite forgotten (which frankly I don't believe) but that Miss did call out to him over the hedge to ask him the time.'

'Surely that is not very likely . . .'

'No, of course not. She would hardly expect him to be wearing a watch, and in any case there were clocks in the cottage, you heard one of them chime the half-hour. I think he simply said the first thing that came into his head, because he could not tell me the truth—and he is not the most brilliant of thinkers. But what had he got to hide? He cannot have been concerned in her disappearance, he was back in the village before half-past two. That young Mrs. Finch thought he was leaving a message. Her husband pointed out that she had nothing to go on, but I think women do sometimes have an instinct over a matter of that sort.'

'And you think it is possible that Octavius might have used Jem as a messenger?'

'Jem is exactly the person he would use. Jem would do anything for Tavy.' She looked a little surprised, and he said: 'In a place of this size, boys are thrown together, whoever their fathers may be. Octavius and Jem became firm allies in their birds-nesting and rock-climbing days. And of course Octavius would rely on him to keep his mouth shut. Say he wanted to visit the cottage when Jack was out of the way . . .'

'He was inside the grounds the whole of that afternoon, wasn't he? Octavius, I mean.'

'My God, so he was! He was in the library when Jack came to tell us that Ada was missing. And he is exactly the kind of person she might have taken up with and then dropped without a scruple. A gentleman, but too young and too poor to be worth cultivating.'

'Could he have killed her, do you think?'

'He might, if she drove him hard enough. I am sorry if it offends you, but it seems most likely to me that the little hussy met the fate she was asking for.'

Caroline remembered the dark-eyed girl in the garden. Death was a terrible retribution at eighteen, no matter what you had done.

'Ada did not appear hard or brazen,' she remarked. 'She was not at all like Betsey to look at, was she?'

'Contrary to the general belief, I never set eyes on her.'

'Oh, I was not aware—I thought you knew them all. She was certainly not a Golden Gainey, and it may have been her darker colouring that made her kind of beauty seem so much less blatant.'

Caroline was facing the window as she spoke. There was a man crossing the lane and coming towards the house.

'Lord Francis, what are we to do? Mr. Charles Richmond is just arriving at the front door.'

He was staring into space, as though his speculations had removed him a thousand miles from his own danger.

'Lord Francis . . .'

'Yes, I heard you. How damnably inopportune, just when I was beginning to see daylight. I'll go out through the dairy and give him the slip.'

It was too late. Richmond was already in the hall. They gazed round the parlour. There was only one possible hiding-place: a cupboard in the wall, in which Mrs. Duffet kept a good deal of spare china. Francis inserted his slim person into the shallow space that was left in front of the soup tureens and sauce boats. He pulled the door towards him. It would not stay shut.

'You'll have to lock me in,' he whispered.

As she turned the key, she heard Richmond already on the point of entering the room. Then Arthur's voice.

'Excuse me, sir. That is a private parlour.'

Explanations from Richmond, a blessed delay, and by the time the two men came in together, Caroline was hunting in the dresser and saying in a busy, auntlike way, 'I cannot think what has happened to Laura's doll.'

'There is not the smallest need,' Mr. Richmond was saying. He looked anxious and unhappy. 'I do not wish to inconvenience any member of your family, sir. I will just have a word with Duffet.'

'My dear sir, we are not entitled to special favours,' replied Arthur, in his most genial manner. 'You have your duty to perform. I don't know where this door leads to . . .'

To Caroline's infinite horror he unlocked the china cupboard.

Then he stood gaping ludicrously at what his public-spirited gesture had revealed.

'You must be Mr. Reed,' said Francis, stepping out of the cupboard with admirable self-command. 'How do you do?'

'Who is this—this person?' demanded Arthur.

'That is Lord Francis Aubrey,' said Charles Richmond, more unhappily than ever.

'Caroline!' exclaimed Arthur. 'You knew he was there —you must have done!'

'Miss Prior was quite unaware of my presence . . .'

'But the key . . .'

'It is a matter of no consequence,' said Francis hastily.

'Well, Charles? I take it you have something to say to me?'

'Yes, sir. That is—I mean—yes.' The special constable cleared his throat, and drew out a sheet of paper, which he unfolded and began to read aloud.

'Francis Alexander FitzMaurice Aubrey, I have here a warrant for your arrest on a charge that you did, on or about the nineteenth day of June in the year of our Lord 1816, at Hoyle Park in the County of Devon, and of your malice aforethought, kill and murder Adelaide Mary Gainey.'

He stopped to take a breath, and Francis asked, 'Have they found the body?'

'Er—no. Not yet.'

'Then you cannot possibly arrest me.'

'There have been cases where no body has been recovered.'

'Yes, when there were sufficient grounds to presume death. But no competent court would accept the hypothesis that Ada Gainey is dead. A woman of her character . . .'

'Such women have just as much right to live as the rest of us!' interposed Charles Richmond hotly.

'So they have, my dear fellow. They also have a much greater independence and freedom of movement than more sheltered women are accustomed to. If one of them chooses to leave her protector without warning, this is a very commonplace event, after all. Why should anyone suppose that she is dead? Mr. Reed, you are a lawyer, I believe.'

'I am thankful to say that I am not your lawyer, my lord,' said Arthur affronted.

'But you owe it to the Lord Chancellor to see that the law is not brought into disrepute by boobies who arrest people for crimes that have never taken place. I don't mean you, Charles; I know you are simply Mansard's agent. I do wish you would consult Mr. Reed about the legal position.'

'That's all very well,' said Richmond. 'How could the girl have gone off to another lover—if that is what you mean—when we know she never left the estate?'

'You don't know anything of the sort,' said Caroline, speaking for the first time. 'She could have gone through the wicket-gate any time around three in the afternoon.'

Richmond was bewildered. 'But surely—are not you the young lady who has been saying all along that this was impossible?'

'I've changed my mind,' she told him airily.

'Caroline, you are a dear girl,' said Francis. 'But I won't have you committing perjury on my behalf.'

'Who gave you leave to address my sister-in-law by her Christian name?'

'My tongue ran away with me. Forgive me, Miss Prior.'

'I'll forgive you,' she said, smiling in spite of herself, 'and I shall not have to commit perjury. I shall simply refuse to give evidence.'

'Then you will probably be sent to prison for contempt of court. Mr. Reed, I am sure it would be better for us all if Richmond were to put that warrant back in his pocket.'

Arthur was at a disadvantage, having only the vaguest idea of the circumstances. When he had been given a brief summary by Charles Richmond, he said that there really was not sufficient evidence to arrest anybody on a charge of murder.

'There is nothing to be gained by being over-hasty. Wait until it is certain that the body of this unfortunate young woman has in fact been buried somewhere on the estate. I am sure that in the meantime Lord Francis will give you his word not to leave Hoyle Park.'

Francis smiled and said nothing. Mr. Richmond was thankful to avoid the necessity of arresting him, even if it was only for a few hours.

Arthur was not going to allow Francis and Caroline the chance to say goodbye or anything else. He hustled her out of the room and up the stairs, scolding her all the way.

'I was never so shocked in my life—a connection of mine, helping a criminal to escape from justice—and don't you be misled by his title, my girl: there is no one more depraved than a black sheep of the aristocracy. You might have had some consideration for my professional standing . . .'

'Arthur, what has happened?' asked Lavinia, peeping nervously out of her bedroom. 'What has Caroline done?'

'I am sorry to tell you, my love, that your sister has behaved very improperly. I caught her hiding Lord Francis Aubrey in a cupboard!'

'Oh dear! Caro, how could you be so—I'm sure she did not mean to do anything improper, Arthur. It is simply that she thinks he is being persecuted.'

Arthur snorted. 'I never saw anyone less like a victim of persecution. And there is no excuse for your behaviour, Caroline. You know how abominably that man treated Lavinia, how could you allow yourself to take his part?'

Caroline would have liked to snap back at Arthur, but she received such an imploring glance from Lavinia that she kept her mouth shut. Mercifully the travelling carriages arrived at that moment, and the lecture came to an end.

Arthur decided to travel in the first post-chaise, with

his wife and his two elder children, leaving Caroline to come in the second with Nurse, Laura, baby Emmie and Horace the pug. This suited her well enough; they were undemanding companions. She was feeling very low as they drove up the combe to the turnpike road, and while their way ran alongside the wall at the back of Hoyle Park she could hardly keep the tears from coming to her eyes.

They had just passed through Brind Abbas, and had not yet changed horses for the first time, when the leading chaise drew up by the roadside, and their own postilions followed suit. Lavinia got out, leading Ben, who wanted to be sick. Arthur followed them, complaining that the child should never have been left to spend all that time on the swing.

'If Caroline had been attending to her duty . . .'

They heard the sound of fast horses coming up behind them. A curricle and pair swung into view. Francis Aubrey was alone in the little open carriage, without a groom. When he caught sight of Caroline he lifted his whip in a gallant salute, and went sailing past them all under a light canopy of dust.

'Did you see that?' exclaimed Arthur, coming up to the door of Caroline's chaise. 'Running away, by God! What could be a clearer confession of guilt? And he's broken his word, into the bargain, which makes his conduct all the more disgraceful.'

'No, he hasn't,' retorted Caroline. 'He's broken your word. You were the one who felt so sure he would remain at Hoyle Park, you never troubled to find out whether he agreed.'

'Why is Papa vexed?' asked Laura.

'Don't ask questions, dear,' said Nurse. 'Let us look out of the window and count how many animals we pass.'

148

So the two yellow post-chaises lumbered on through the Devon valleys, Nurse and Laura chronicled dogs and ducks and cows, and Caroline sat wondering what to make of that last glimpse of Francis in the curricle.

Perhaps Octavius had already left Cleave, and he had decided to go in pursuit. That must be it. Because otherwise his own departure did look uncommonly like a confession of guilt.

## 17

The Reeds reached London on Saturday evening, and were to remain there about ten days before going on to the new lodgings at Ramsgate. Sunday and Monday passed slowly. There was continued speculation about Ada's fate in the public prints, but no fresh news.

On Tuesday Caroline went out to match a skein of embroidery silk. She was badly in need of air. The Reeds' house, like their marriage, seemed to be full of unnecessary furniture and short of any sort of mental stimulus. She strolled in Lincoln's Inn Fields, watching the pale London children on the drab London grass, and imagining the dazzling, foam-crusted sea rushing up the beach at Martland.

She slackened her pace a little each time she passed the tall house occupied by Mr. William Parminter, wondering whether he knew why Francis had left Cleave and where he was now. Presently Mr Parminter's clerk came out of the house, a very respectable man whom Caroline knew by sight, and she studied him with heightened interest; he had become absurdly important to her simply because of his tenuous connection with Francis.

You must be mad, she admonished herself, and was about to walk on, when the clerk came up to her and said: 'Mr. Parminter's compliments, ma'am. He would be very much obliged if you could spare him a few minutes.'

She could hardly believe her luck. 'I should be delighted to do so.'

The ground floor of Mr. Parminter's house was very much like their own. She was conducted into a lofty, rather dark room where the lawyer was sitting at a table covered with papers. He rose to his feet.

'Miss Prior, I must beg your indulgence for having approached you in such a very odd manner . . .'

'That does not signify in the least, sir. Only tell me, if you please—do you know what has happened to Lord Francis Aubrey?'

'You will be pleased to hear—I hope you will be pleased to hear that Lord Francis is in excellent health,' said a well-known voice behind her.

She turned quickly, and there he was, standing in front of a high bookcase and smiling at her: slight, alert and resilient as ever.

'Oh, I am so glad . . .'

'Did you think I was under lock and key? Old Mansard seems to have got cold feet, and no one here is anxious to issue a warrant, even though Eltham is now in London, trying to stir up trouble. They still haven't found a body.'

'Why did you . . .' began Caroline; she was going to ask, why did you run away, but changed it to: 'Why did you want to see me?'

'To enlist your help. Which perhaps I ought not to do,

after the scrape I got you into by hiding in the china cupboard. Is poor Reed still on the verge of apoplexy?'

'He says you are a black sheep of the aristocracy.'

Francis burst out laughing, and Mr. Parminter looked scandalised. Oh dear, thought Caroline, this wretched man is leading me astray; I am beginning to say outrageous things just for the fun of it.

'Perhaps I should inform you,' said Mr. Parminter, 'that this business has had more distressing consequences for Lord Francis than he cares to admit. He receives a daily budget of insulting anonymous letters, he has been threatened in the street, and he finds it embarrassing to enter his clubs.'

'I am so sorry,' said Caroline, abashed.

'Never mind that,' said Francis briefly. 'Are you prepared to accompany me and Mr. Parminter on a journey of discovery? It is hardly any distance, and I should be uncommonly grateful.'

'I think you ought to tell Miss Prior a little more than that,' remarked Mr. Parminter.

'Well, I don't intend to. I don't wish to influence her in any way.

Caroline said at once that she was perfectly ready to go with them. She was extremely curious to know what he wanted from her, but she did not ask.

A carriage was now waiting at the door. They got into it and were driven away, Caroline wondering whether Arthur was looking out of his window.

She was surprised when they turned eastwards in the direction of the City. Neither of the men spoke. Francis seemed preoccupied and perhaps nervous. The drive soon ended in the yard of an inn somewhere behind Fleet Street. They all got out. There were a couple of short-stage coaches

151

taking on passengers. One had the inscription: Paddington. The other read: Blackwall—East India Docks. There was an air of energetic confusion. People hurried about with baskets and parcels; waiters hurried after them with refreshments on trays. Caroline could not imagine why she had been brought here; surely they were not going on a public coach to Paddington? But Francis led the way into the inn.

'No need to enquire,' he said to Mr. Parminter. 'It's the last door on the left at the end of the passage, according to Jones.'

No one paid any attention to them, and as they set off along this passage Caroline suddenly grasped the significance of a coach that was going to the East India Dock. She thought of Octavius Barrow who had spoken of joining the army. Perhaps India offered an alternative means of escape. When they stopped at the last door on the left, she was sure Octavius was going to be on the other side of it.

Francis knocked, and opened the door without waiting for an invitation. There was a man sitting just inside, someone Caroline had never seen before; he was tall and well-built, about thirty years old and not in the least like Octavius. Her glance flicked over him and then on to the other occupant of the room, who was silhouetted against the window.

'So we meet again,' said Francis with great cordiality. 'Miss Prior, may I present Mr. and Mrs. Finch.'

Caroline was staring at the girl by the window.

'That's not Mrs. Finch,' she said in a voice of total incredulity. 'That's Ada Gainey.'

'I'm delighted to hear you say so, for I'd come to the conclusion that it must be.'

## 18

The young man called Finch was trying to turn them out.

'You've no right in here,' he said fiercely. 'I've hired this room and paid for it, and you have no authority to come pestering us. What crime are we guilty of?'

'Causing a public mischief,' said Mr. Parminter.

'What?'

'There have been dozens of men out searching for Miss Gainey for the past fourteen days, neglecting the urgent work of their farms. There might also be a charge of abduction; you are not married, I think?'

'That's not my fault,' retorted Finch, angry and resentful. 'We intend to marry as soon as we can do so without attracting notice. While all this fuss has been going on I dared not apply for a licence.'

'So you are attempting to take a minor out of the country without the consent of her parents.'

'My parents have consented to worse things than that,' said the girl scornfully.

Caroline thought Finch was going to attack Mr. Parminter. 'Don't you threaten me with that kind of legal hypocrisy,' he told the lawyer. 'Do you know that Ada's mother sold her to her first well-connected seducer when she was fifteen years old? If you take me to court, I'll start such a scandal . . .'

'No one is taking you to court,' said Francis, who was leaning against the closed door in a deceptively casual manner. 'You can go abroad—get married—do what you like—so long as you understand that this business must be cleared up before you go. Ada, I want a properly attested statement, if you please, saying that you left Hoyle Park of your own free will, and without any intimidation from me.'

She stared at him. 'Why should I give you that?'

'Because there is a warrant out for my arrest on a charge of murder, and if you continue to be so confoundedly disobliging, I shall be tempted to make a true bill of it.'

Here, unexpectedly, Ada giggled.

'A warrant for your arrest?' repeated Finch, disconcerted and a good deal less belligerent. 'Well, I'm sorry, my lord—I can see it must be very inconvenient for you, but what are we to do? If Ada signs a statement that is shown to her family, they will separate us and stop our marriage. They'd never agree to her marrying anyone like me; why do you think we ran away in the first place? They can ruin me if they want to, they have many powerful friends. There is a post waiting for me in Portugal, but my employer might be persuaded to dismiss me; if you are a wine importer you cannot afford to offend your best customers.'

'Well, if it comes to that,' said Francis, 'I am a good customer to my own wine merchant, and so are quite a number of my friends. I reckon there are men in Oporto who would be pleased to acquire your services, come what may.' Finch and Ada exchanged glances of surprise and speculation, but he affected not to notice this, and went on talking to them both. 'These fears of retribution seem to me greatly exaggerated. I think your family will be so thankful to know that you are safe, Ada, that they will let you marry anyone you choose. Did you know that your mother has had some kind of seizure?'

There was a slight pause.

'Has she?' said Ada in a hard little voice. 'I'm sure I don't care.'

'And Hester, last time I saw her, had been shedding tears on your account. That is an achievement you may be proud of. None of her lovers has ever made Hester cry. And Betsey has gone to Devonshire to look for you.'

Caroline had heard all this in growing confusion; she thought the most important point had been overlooked. 'It's all very well to talk of getting married and going to Portugal, but what have they done with the real Mrs. Finch? Did they—is it her body that is buried in the wood?'

Everyone tried to speak at once.

'Come, Caroline—this is not up to your usual performance,' said Francis, who was now obviously enjoying himself. 'Have you not perceived the beauty of the scheme? There never was a real Mrs. Finch or a body in the wood.'

'Then who was the lady who entered the Wilderness with Mr. Finch at the Martland end?'

'Did anyone ever see this mysterious lady?'

'No, but the groom . . . Oh!'

'Was a groom for that one occasion only, I fancy.' Francis glanced enquiringly at Finch.

'Yes, sir. He's a friend of mine, an actor. We worked out the whole plan together.'

Somehow the atmosphere had become friendly, almost social. Mr. Parminter was a little put out by Caroline's presence, and said that perhaps she would like to wait in the carriage, but Caroline pretended not to hear, and sat down by Francis on a small stiff sofa. Gilbert Finch perched on the edge of the table, with Ada on a stool beside him. Mr. Parminter took the only chair.

The runaways were suddenly eager to tell their story. They had met for the first time four months ago, when Ada was living with her previous lover in Half Moon Street. A case of inferior wine had been delivered by mistake; Gilbert had been sent round from Baldock and Scroggs to apologise. The master of the house was out, but he saw Ada. It was as though they had both been struck by the same flash of lightning. They abandoned all the very different advice that each had been given by a prudent family. They began meeting in secret, and soon decided that nothing less than marriage would satisfy their love for each other. This meant that they would have to leave London for a variety of good reasons. Gilbert had a friend with connections in Portugal. There was a vacancy out there for a man who already knew the English side of the business. It would take a few weeks to make all the arrangements and fix up a sea-passage; in the meantime Ada quarrelled deliberately with Mr. Oatley and went to stay with Betsey. She and Gilbert were planning to be married by licence but not to go off together until the day they actually stepped on to the ship. In that way they would be safe from discovery or pursuit.

Various men had began to cast out lures for Ada; but it was easy enough to turn them down—the Gainey sisters prided themselves on being particular in their choice of lovers; it was this degree of fastidiousness which separated a courtesan from an ordinary kept woman. So all went well until she found herself faced with a prospect which it was virtually impossible for her to refuse; a young nobleman not simply agreeable and considerate, but also romantic, high-minded and a bachelor in need of a wife.

'It was such a waste,' lamented Ada. 'Why couldn't he have taken up with Sally or Betsey? Why did it have to be me? I did try to send him away; I know Gilbert thinks I didn't try hard enough . . .'

'I never said that, my love.'

'You thought it, and you were right. But it was not Eltham that I couldn't resist; it was Mama and Hester, watching me and telling me what I must do. I have always been afraid of Mama, and of Hester too, in a different way. She is so quick and clever and determined. You can't have any privacy in my family, everyone interferes and criticises, and they care only for settlements and titles.'

Gilbert took her hand and held it, and she continued in a firmer voice.

'I made myself as tiresome to poor Eltham as I could. I found he had no money, so I insisted that I wanted a house—and then he carried me off to that cottage, the horridest place under all those dismal trees. And I must say, Lord Francis, that I think the man who built it was mad.'

'He was my great-grandfather and you are not alone in your opinion.'

Ada had been nearly desperate, she said, until Gilbert and his actor friend Daniel arrived in the neighbourhood on the Saturday before her escape. They paid a discreet visit to the cottage in order to work out a plan, which was dominated by their obsessive fear of Ada's family. None of her sisters was aware of Gilbert's existence, but a few people in London did know what had been going on, and if Ada was seen leaving the village with a strange young man, she was sure Hester would put two and two together, and start making the sort of enquiries which would identify him in the end. How much better if she was to vanish in such a way that all attempts to find her would be centred around Hoyle Park.

'We thought it might seem as though I had been drowned,' she said calmly. 'Or perhaps fallen down a quarry.'

So on that fateful Tuesday afternoon Daniel, disguised as a groom parted from Gilbert at the top of Martland combe and drove the gig to the Ship in Cleave, where he talked a good deal about his master and mistress, whom he had left exploring the Wilderness. In the meantime Gilbert walked down the combe and through the wicket-gate; it was then about ten minutes past one. He took with him a bonnet and shawl for Ada—she needed to wear something that no one in the village had seen before—and also a pair of half-boots, more suitable for the Wilderness than her usual flimsy shoes. Ada was looking out for him; she hid him out of sight and presently got rid of Molly. She then sat down in front of the cottage and waited for a suitable passer-by to play the innocent witness who was a necessary member of their cast. The first person to come along was Jem Heard. She called out to him, asking him the time, simply to fix her presence in his mind.

At this point in her narrative, Ada paused and glanced at Francis. 'When you came to Kentish Town, you said that he denied having spoken to me. I can't imagine why.'

'I dare say he may have been nervous or embarrassed; he probably admired you and was afraid of being chaffed by his friends. Nothing more sinister than that.'

'Yes, that might be so. At all events, we decided he would suit our purpose, and as soon as he was gone I put on my bonnet and we hurried after him.'

'So promptly,' remarked Francis, 'that you found you were carrying your white kid shoes in your hand, and you had to stop and bury them.'

Ada and Gilbert regarded him as though he was a sorcerer.

'How did you know . . . ?'

'You don't mean to say they've dug up Ada's shoes?'

'Yes, and very disagreeable they looked. Poor Betsey nearly fainted at the sight of them.'

'Betsey never faints!' exclaimed Ada, but she did look rather stricken all the same. She soon went on with her story.

'We followed that young Jem Heard, talking and laughing to make sure he knew we were there. He turned round once, and that was all we needed. And as we were congratulating ourselves on our success, I got a fright; a little pug-dog came running up to us from the direction of the village, and it was the one I had seen several times in the wood with that young lady.' She addressed Caroline. 'I thought you must be quite close by, and I was sure you would recognise me, because you must have seen me so very clearly, that morning we passed you coming away from Eltham House. I whispered to Gilbert, and we stepped off the path and tried to get out of sight behind the trees, only they were rather thin just there. So we turned back and kept on walking until we heard you calling the dog, and by then we were level with the cottage once again. I had a splendid idea. I pulled off my bonnet and shawl, thrust them at Gilbert and told him to stay where he was. Then I ran round into the front garden and I was sitting on my chair once more when you arrived with those children and caught the pug.'

'So that's how you managed to be in two places at once —or I should say, two people at once.' Caroline thought this over. 'I saw you in the garden at half-past two . . . Why were we all so convinced that Mr. Finch and his companion had already left the village? Did not Mrs. Harper say so?'

'No,' said Francis. 'She simply said they came out of the wood after Jem Heard. Eventually I had the wit to ask her, how long after? She told me there was a difference of at least twenty minutes.'

'We never thought of anyone keeping such an exact watch on the gate,' said Gilbert. 'We walked through the wood a second time without any further mishap, and found the gig waiting just outside. We were not in the village street above a minute and we reckoned that Ada's face was pretty well hidden by that great bonnet; very few people in Cleave had ever seen her properly, apart from two or three of Eltham's servants. Still, we were running no risks. We got into the gig and drove away as fast as we could.'

'Very neat,' said Mr. Parminter. 'Very neat indeed.' He had apparently forgotten the more dubious aspects of their adventure. 'You'd have got clean away, we could never have traced you. For heaven's sake, man—what possessed you to write me that letter? Why couldn't you leave well alone?'

'You are wrong,' said Francis, before Gilbert could answer. 'We could have traced him, and he knew it, didn't you, Finch? Your friend somewhat overplayed the part of the talkative groom. He did not actually leave your name with Sam Roebuck at the Ship, but he said you worked for a wine merchant in Duke Street.'

'Yes, and he was in a terrible taking, poor fellow. I might have known something of the sort would happen. Actors!' said Gilbert ruefully. 'Still, it wasn't entirely his fault. He went to the inn on purpose to chatter about his employers to anyone who would listen, how his mistress was fond of botanising and romantic scenery and so forth —so that when they saw us drive off in the gig, they'd think of us both as flesh-and-blood visitors who had arrived in the village that very afternoon. It had never dawned on any of us that strangers who walked through the Wilderness were expected to go into the Ship as a matter of course. Daniel knew we could not afford to do so, for fear Ada might be recognised, yet at the same time he saw that our going straight on, without taking any kind of refreshment, and on such a very hot day, might later be thought suspicious. He could not devise any excuse, on the spur of the moment, except that my being in the wine trade had made me particular about what I ate and drank—of course this was all nonsense, but it didn't matter, for the innkeeper was so disgruntled that he didn't want our custom. Only then it dawned on Daniel that he had spoken a little too freely about the nature of my employment in London.

'At first I saw no reason for alarm—I didn't see why we should ever be suspected—but soon the rumours began in the newspapers, and it occurred to us that Ada's friends might start trying to trace everyone who had been in the vicinity of Hoyle Park that day, simply as a last resort. If they came to Duke Street—well, there have been a few difficulties lately at the shop; I was supposed to be ill bed all the time I was in Devonshire, but I felt certain Mr. Scroggs had begun to smell a rat.'

'So you did not want anyone round making enquiries,' said Mr. Parminter. 'I understand that. You thought it would be wiser to prevent that if you could?'

'Yes, sir. Ada knew you were Lord Eltham's man of affairs, and I hoped a letter to you might convince everyone that I had nothing more to tell. If you still wanted to see me, I thought you would write and ask me to call at your chambers. It never entered my head that anyone would search me out at my private address, and when Lord Francis appeared in Kentish Town—I can tell you, my lord, it was the most disagreeable shock I ever had in my life!'

'You carried off the whole situation with great skill—though I think the honours go to your accomplice. Young Mrs. Finch who described the elusive Miss Gainey as a hussy—and who shall say that she was wrong?' added Francis, staring very straight at Ada. 'A fine fool you made of me, the pair of you.'

Ada gave him a ravishing smile. 'You are a true sportsman to take it so well. Of course I'll sign that paper if you want me to. Provided Gilbert and I can go abroad directly afterwards.'

'I hope you will be willing to meet your family before you go.'

Ada looked mulish. 'I don't wish to meet them. I don't ever want to see them again. They are nothing to me.'

'I am sorry to hear that; you still mean a great deal to your parents and sisters, who are suffering at this moment because they believe you are dead. If they learn the truth without a word from you to soften it, I think they will continue to suffer in a different way, for I am sure they all love you. My dear child, do consider this very carefully: how will you feel, out there in a foreign country, when perhaps you are starting your own nursery, if you have cut yourself off for ever from Hester and Sally and Betsey?'

Caroline was amazed by the gentleness of his manner, his real concern for Ada and her family. Ada herself was not proof against this appeal. Her mouth trembled a little, and she was perhaps on the brink of relenting when there was a commotion in the passage outside.

The door was flung open by Jack Eltham, flushed and furious, with Mr. Parminter's clerk in hot pursuit.

'He got the direction out of Jones,' gasped the clerk. 'I did try to stop him!'

Jack pushed his way towards Ada. 'My beloved, thank God you are alive! What have these villains done to you?'

Gilbert Finch placed himself solidly in the way, and Jack, trying to grapple with him, caught sight of Francis. 'I knew you were at the bottom of this!' he shouted. 'You thought you could abduct her—have her smuggled out of the country—do you mean to call off your hired bully, or shall I fetch a constable?'

'You are a little too hasty about fetching constables. And I should take care how you speak of Mr. Gilbert Finch. He is the man Miss Gainey is going to marry.'

'So that's the game, is it? A forced marriage! If you dare to lay hands on her, you scoundrel . . .'

Gilbert hit him, fairly hard, and he went staggering back against the wall, knocking over a small table and a brass candlestick. Ada and Francis both moved forward instinctively. They met in the cramped space: Francis put a hand under her elbow to steady her, and said:

'You will have to tell him yourself, you know. He won't accept it from anyone else.'

Jack was straightening up and rubbing his chin. He said 'Ada?' on a note of sudden apprehension.

'I am not being abducted, Eltham,' she said in a low voice. 'Your uncle had nothing to do with . . . He only found us this morning. I left Devonshire of my own free will; I never intended to stay there. I was already engaged to Gilbert when I first met you.'

Dumb with shock Jack stared first at Ada and then at the scowling Gilbert—no fashionable Adonis, but a man five years older than himself and three inches taller, with a sort of steady strength; unmistakably his successful rival. As he faced them, the whole horror of his own situation, the part he had played in their lives, seemed to sweep over him.

'Why did you come to me?' he whispered. 'You cannot have wanted—you must have hated me.'

'You were so very kind,' she said with some compunction. 'And I have played you a shabby trick in return. I'm sorry, Eltham.'

'But why didn't you send me away? I can't understand it. I would never importune a girl who did not care for me.'

Ada did not answer.

It was Francis who said, 'What sort of treatment do you think she would have had from her family if she had turned down a chance of becoming the Marchioness of Eltham?'

Jack looked startled, and then more wretched than before.

'You must remember,' said Francis, 'in all these houses where you are received with such flattering complacency, that the mothers probably like you better than their daughters do. This is a useful lesson in humility.'

It was also an extraordinarily heartless thing to say at such a moment. Even so, Caroline could forgive Francis for saying it; she was sure he was recalling his own unhappy pursuit of Lavinia.

## 19

'How could she play such a cruel trick on us?' exclaimed Hester. ''Cause a public outcry, treat Eltham so badly, nearly kill my mother—and all because she wants to run

off to live in Portugal with a wretched shopkeeper. I am
thoroughly ashamed of her!'

'But you will agree to see her before she goes,' pleaded
Sally. 'And the young man. I own I am very curious to see
him.'

'We don't yet know whether she is prepared to come
here. Is she, Francis?'

'She'll come,' said Francis.

He was standing in front of the fireplace in the Mount
Street drawing-room, contemplating his polished hessians.
He had driven here directly from the coaching inn to tell
the Gaineys that Ada was alive, and the task had been a
difficult one. Hester and Sally were both so bewildered
and distressed when they finally understood that their little
sister had rejected them.

'She'll come,' he repeated. 'Only you must not scold
her, Hester. She's frightened of you. That's why she ran
away.'

'Frightened? Of me? You cannot be serious.' Hester
glanced once more at the short, bald note that lay on the
table. '. . . *I am in good health and am shortly to be married* . . .' 'She sounds perfectly brazen about it.'

'Whistling in the dark,' said Francis laconically.

'Oh. Do you think—I am in the dark, I can tell you
that,' said Hester. 'And whatever I have done wrong in my
life I never meant anything but good towards Ada. It
seems hard that she should be the one to hurt me so much.'

'We have all been at cross-purposes,' said Sally. 'You
will forgive her the moment you see her, I know you will.
Lord Francis is going to bring her to us—how grateful we
are to you, Lord Francis. You have been a veritable angel
in disguise.'

'Charming of you to say so, Miss Sally. The disguise is

generally thought to be impenetrable.'

'An angel heaping coals of fire, I imagine,' said Hester, smiling for the first time.

'Not at all,' he replied. 'We have a good deal in common. Your sister cannot think worse of you than my nephew thinks of me.'

When he left them, a few minutes later, he went round to Eltham House, where he was told that the Marquess was not at home. He called at five, and again after dinner, but still Jack had not returned. On his third visit he settled himself in the small saloon and waited. It was not until one in the morning that he decided to end his vigil, and set out down Berkeley Street and along Piccadilly to Albany.

Whatever the hour, that part of London was never at rest. There were late carriages, their jogging lamps reflected in the rainy street; tipsy wayfarers straggling across the pavement, pale shapes of drabs and prostitutes lurked in the shadows; waltz music poured from a lighted window. And in all those rows of prosperous houses, so many disastrous pleasures available to a disillusioned young man who was too unhappy to go home.

Francis was wearing a rather grim expression as he entered the hallowed precincts of Albany and climbed the stairs to his own chambers. His servant was waiting up for him.

'The Marquess has been wanting to see you, my lord. Very anxious for a word with you. He came round soon after nine.'

Francis stood still. 'I never thought of that. How long ago did he leave?'

'He's still here, my lord. Fast asleep.'

Francis went into the high, quiet room where his collection of Chinese porcelain glowed mutely in the candle-light. Jack was lolling sideways in a wing chair; he was haggard from strain and exhaustion, but still managed to look extraordinarily young. His uncle touched him lightly on the arm.

Jack opened his eyes, blinked in a puzzled way, and then the whole of the immediate past surged back into his mind. He jerked himself upright, saying: 'I beg your pardon, how stupid of me. I was so anxious to speak to you, and I thought I would stay until you came in.'

'While I have been round in Berkeley Square, waiting for you.' Francis glanced about him. 'Didn't Simpson bring you any refreshment?'

'Oh, he offered me everything in your cellar. But I didn't want to get drunk.'

'What admirable self-command. If I were in your shoes, I should be as drunk as a wheelbarrow by now.'

'I felt I ought to stay sober long enough to apologise,' said Jack, who was now standing up and preparing to make a speech. 'I am fully sensible, my lord, of having done you a grave injustice, which I deeply regret, and which in time I hope you will find it possible to overlook —though I don't see how you are going to overlook my having called you a murderer,' he added, coming down with a bump from his Johnsonian heights. 'It isn't the sort of thing that slips one's memory.'

'You will feel better now you have got that off your chest,' said Francis.

He fetched a decanter and two glasses from a cupboard, poured out some port and handed one of the glasses to Jack, who took a reviving swig and nearly choked.

'There is one thing I should like to ask you,' said Francis, gazing thoughtfully into his glass. 'According to what you said that evening in the orangery, you have spent the last few years under the impression that I was stealing from the estate. Is this true?'

'No, sir—I assure you! I hardly knew what I was saying, and I am extremely sorry . . .'

'Well, I am glad to hear it,' said Francis bluntly. 'If you had gone on for three or four years believing that you were being robbed and doing nothing whatever about it, I really think I should have washed my hands of you altogether, Eltham. There is a limit to the stupidity one can endure, even from relations.'

'Oh!' said Jack, startled by this unorthodox response. He thought it over, and took another sip of port. 'I am afraid I must have reached the limits of your endurance long ago . . . But as to what I said in the orangery, I never had the smallest suspicion until quite lately; it was while I was down in Devonshire with time on my hands, and people kept saying there was money being taken out of the estate that was never put back, then I did begin to wonder. So that when—when Ada disappeared, I let the whole business prey on my mind.'

'It was a pity you could not have consulted Sturdy, your own steward. Instead of listening to the maunderings of old Mansard, as reported by Octavius.'

'Yes, I know that now,' said Jack in a low voice. 'It's what Parminter said this afternoon, when he told me where the money had really gone to.'

'Parminter? I hope he took Caroline Prior back to her sister's, as I asked him to?'

'What? Oh yes, I believe so. In fact I know he did, for he was going there first, and he made such a point of my calling on him afterwards. I wandered around for a while, feeling too wretched to care what became of me, and at last I thought I might as well go and see what Parminter wanted.

'He told me a lot that I didn't understand before. Of the ruinous condition things were in when my father died, half the income going to pay his debts, and how you were hard put to it, even to keep a roof on Dillingford. He says you have at last got us out of the doldrums by building streets of new houses on the London property, and letting them at a high rent.'

'It was the only sensible plan, even though it meant a good deal of cheeseparing. Houses don't get built for nothing. That's why the timber from Lancross Wood had to be sold.'

'Yes, I understand that now. Parminter says you even risked your own private inheritance . . .'

'Well, that was not such a very heroic transaction, and I have already made a great deal of money out of it.' Francis brushed aside all Jack's expressions of gratitude, saying, 'I am a natural speculator. I enjoy it, although it is not considered a gentlemanly pursuit. Your father was a gamester. You knew that, didn't you?'

'I knew he had lost a great deal at play; I had no idea of the real extent—I suppose you did not want me to know. You were very much attached to my father, weren't you, sir?'

'He was the best friend I ever had,' said Francis promptly. 'However, I would not have concealed his faults from you through some false notion of loyalty. The truth is far less romantic. I knew it would be easier for me to go on dealing with the financial problems on my own, and as you never showed the faintest interest in the management of your estates, I was too selfish to undertake the labour of instructing you. A state of affairs that does not reflect much credit on either of us.'

'I am sorry you thought I wasn't interested, Uncle Francis,' said Jack, at the end of a longish pause. 'I did try—just after I left Eton—to find out a little. I expect I was very dull, because you bit my head—I mean, you made it clear that you would get on better without me.'

'So I bit your head off? Did you mind very much? Yes, I see you did. How I sympathise with Hester.'

'I beg your pardon, sir?' Jack looked puzzled.

'We must make another attempt. I will try to initiate you in a rather less churlish manner. You will soon get the hang of things.'

'It's very kind of you, sir,' said Jack in a mournful voice. 'I expect it will occupy my mind.'

Francis smiled slightly. 'The summer of your life is not entirely over, you know.'

Jack said nothing.

'I have not mentioned the other matter,' said Francis, speaking with unusual sensibility, 'because I know what a painful subject it must be. But don't imagine that I am indifferent. Just remember that she is very young—which partly accounts for an action of such wanton unkindness —and try to forgive her if you can. For your own sake. The bitterness of despised love can be so destructive.'

'I don't feel any bitterness towards Ada. It's myself I can't forgive, my own vanity and greed. To have caused her such anguish, forced her to take me against her inclination; it's too horrible to think of ...'

He could not stop thinking of it all the same, and talking of it too, once he had started, and after a while he was no longer surprised to find himself confiding in Francis, whose cold-water judgments and scathing tongue had always disconcerted him.

And Francis, listening, thought: I couldn't have taken such a blow like this. In fact I didn't. He's got a more generous spirit than most of us.

Jack would be none the worse in the long run, and the time would come when he would be grateful to the girl for not marrying him.

But even Francis had the sense not to tell him so.

## 20

'I will not have that fellow in my house!' declared Arthur, waving aside the card which the parlourmaid had offered him on a salver. 'I consider it a great impertinence his coming here at all.'

'Why should he not come?' asked Caroline in a mutinous voice. 'There is no longer the slightest chance of his being arrested for murder.'

'That is not exactly a passport to respectability,' said Arthur heavily humorous. 'I have no desire to entertain everybody in London who is *not* a murderer.'

'Oh, Arthur,' said Lavinia, her large eyes troubled. 'Do you not think someone ought to see him?'

'Certainly not. I'm surprised at your suggesting such a thing. Well, Boulter'—to the parlourmaid—'what are you waiting for?'

'What am I to say to the gentleman, if you please, sir?'

'You may tell him that your mistress is not at home, and that she is going out of town for the rest of the summer.'

'Very good, sir.'

Boulter departed, and Lavinia took the opportunity to creep out of the room after her, as Caroline noticed with a flash of irritation and contempt. Lavinia could not sustain even the small part of a neutral witness in the arguments that kept breaking out between her husband and her sister.

Left alone with Arthur, Caroline gritted her teeth and prepared to endure in silence yet one more repetition of the scolding she had been given two days ago when she returned from her expedition with Francis and Mr. Parminter.

'. . . Shocking impropriety . . . shameless association with a man whose very name ought to be abhorrent to you . . . behaving like a chit out of the schoolroom . . .'

She swallowed it all without answering back, and was rewarded for this self-denial by Arthur telling her not to sulk.

'You need not look daggers at me, miss. I am speaking purely for your own good. Now I must not delay any longer, I have to go to Grosvenor Street to read Sir Matthew Clifton's will. You may tell your sister that I shall probably be out until dinner-time.'

Arthur bustled off importantly, leaving Caroline to fight back the tears that sprang into her eyes all too often. She leant against the chimney-piece, and saw her face reflected in the glass: glum and plain, almost the face of a stranger. She had been feeling ill with unhappiness and anxiety ever since they got back from Devonshire, and to know that Francis had actually come to the house, and that Arthur had sent him away was more than she could bear.

She was making for the privacy of her own room when Lavinia re-appeared, still visibly agitated.

'Caro, where are you going?'

'Upstairs.'

'Oh. I wish you would stay down here a little longer.'

'Why?' asked Caroline disagreeably. 'Do you want to read me another lecture?'

'I gave Boulter a message for Lord Francis. I said he could come back as soon as he saw Arthur leave the house.'

'Vin, I cannot believe it!' gasped Caroline.

'Well, it's true,' said Lavinia distractedly. 'I know it was wrong of me to disobey Arthur's wishes, but I owe Lord Francis some kind of reparation, and now I am older I understand that he is not as bad as I thought—at least, I do hope not. And you have been so unhappy, Caro— if only I am doing what is best for you. It is so difficult to be sure—and I cannot imagine what Boulter must be thinking.'

'I am sure she is delighted. You know she dotes on the nobility.'

At which moment Boulter opened the drawing-room door with a flourish, and announced: 'Lord Francis Aubrey, ma'am.'

'My dear Mrs. Reed, this is very kind of you.'

He held out his hand to Lavinia, who took it with a good deal of confusion.

'Lord Francis, I hardly know what to say! I am afraid my husband has not been at all—he has a totally false notion of your character, and that is due to my want of resolution, for I have never told him the true facts about the ending of our—our former acquaintance.'

'Of course you did not. It would have been folly to do so,' said Francis cheerfully. 'No one wants to rake up the past.'

'You are generous,' said Lavinia, pink with embarrass-ment. 'I felt you had the right to come here and tell Caroline how you unravelled the mystery, which she is dying to hear. But I must warn you that I could not connive at a second visit. Everything that needs to be said must be said today.'

'I understand you perfectly,' he assured her.

Caroline, watching them, thought: how could she jilt him for that insipid Alfred? And must she not regret the past, comparing him with Arthur? He was very well turned out today in his dark blue coat and dove coloured panta-loons; they were so perfectly cut to fit his slight figure that he looked positively elegant.

Lavinia had gone, they were alone.

'Well, my fellow conspirator,' said Francis. 'I am sorry I have once again landed you in a scrape with your brother-in-law.'

'Oh, that doesn't signify! I don't care what he thinks. Only it has been very tantalising not knowing the end of the story—or even the middle of the story, for when I last saw you in Cleave, you thought Ada must be dead, and we were wondering whether Octavius could have killed her.'

'Octavius! Yes, you thought he was suffering from pangs of conscience, did you not? A very astute surmise.'

'But surely he had no hand in Ada's elopement?'

'No, he was nursing a different secret altogether. You remember the paragraph in the *St. James's Chronicle*? Octavius wrote that.'

Caroline gazed at him in astonishment.

'The little monster!' she said indignantly. 'How could he act so maliciously towards the members of a family who had always befriended him? It is quite shocking.'

'I suspect he did it to earn a few guineas. He and Jack had been working on each other's imagination—you know what a gossip he is—and I fancy he strung together all the most hair-raising rumours he could collect without fully understanding how they would read in print or what a stir they would create. No wonder he was frightened; it wasn't the sight of Ada's shoes that alarmed him, it was my saying I intended to make enquiries at the post office.'

'Yes, of course,' she said slowly. 'I suppose he almost hoped you would be arrested before you had the chance. And yet at the same time he felt it was partly his fault. What will you do? And how did you find out?'

'Now that Ada is known to be alive, I have been able to demand a grovelling apology from the editor of the *Chronicle*, and one of the terms I insisted on was the name of their correspondent in Devonshire. I am writing Master Octavius a pretty severe letter, I can tell you. If I get a suitably chastened reply, I shall let the matter drop. He must have been feeling fairly uncomfortable for the last week, not knowing if his secret would be uncovered, and I hope it will have taught him a lesson. No sense in dragging in the Rector.'

'No, he would be so distressed, poor old man.'

'Whenever Tavy does anything that annoys him, he starts talking about David and Absalom, and really it puts one quite out of countenance. Besides, I can't persecute that silly boy while Ada herself is getting off scot free.'

Caroline noted that he had his own standards of justice, as you would expect. Dismissing Octavius from her mind, she turned to the more fascinating subject of Ada.

'How did you decide she was in London after all? What made you change your mind?'

'You did.'

'I? But I had not the least idea . . .'

'You expressed surprise, that morning at the farm, when

I said I had never met Ada. Until then I had somehow assumed, without giving the matter much thought, that I should be bound to recognise her if I saw her. I knew she was darker than her sisters, but in spite of this I was convinced that she was exactly like them—and they are all four remarkably like each other. Even as you convinced me that this was a fallacy, I thought of a young woman connected with the case, and vouched for by no one except the man who claimed to be her husband. From then on it was easy.'

'No wonder you were so particularly anxious not to be arrested at that point.'

'It would have been fatal. As soon as I got rid of Richmond, I visited Mrs. Harper and made sure that my new theory was feasible as far as times and places went. Then I set out immediately for London.'

'I went straight to Baldock and Scroggs, but I was too late. Finch had left his employment, and his lodgings, the day after I called on him. This made me more certain than ever that the girl I had seen in Kentish Town was Ada Gainey—especially when the people at the shop assured me that Finch was unmarried. One of the men there believed that he was planning to seek his fortune on the Continent, and I must say my heart sank a little at this news, for if they had already gone abroad it was going to be almost impossible to dispel the rumour that I had somehow disposed of Ada. Even though they never found a body. All I could do was to hope that Gilbert and Ada had gone into hiding because they had been frightened by my visit (which seemed reasonable) and that they had not yet left the country. I consulted Parminter, and we set about finding them.'

'But how could you expect to do so, in a town the size of

London? It sounds an impossible task, and I can't think how you accomplished it.'

'We had one straw to clutch. If Gilbert and Ada had not yet gone abroad, it must be because they were waiting for a passage that had been arranged for them on one particular vessel. They would therefore have to keep themselves informed about her sailing date, when and where they were to board her, and so forth. We made enquiries among the wine-shippers and other agents, we looked for them at Gravesend, and at various likely places, and also at the short-stage coaching inns. There are around thirty coaches a day plying between the City and the Port, and anyone frequenting such a place could find out all he wanted to know about the movements of ships.

'On Tuesday morning Parminter's junior clerk discovered a couple calling themselves Mr. and Mrs. Field who answered to the description of Gilbert and Ada in every detail. Parminter and I were determined to confront them immediately, but neither of us knew Ada by sight, and if the young woman insisted that she was somebody quite different we were hardly in a position to contradict her. We needed a witness who would recognise Ada. We weren't very anxious to take either Jack or any of the Gaineys. You were the ideal choice. Parminter said I should never have dragged you into such a ramshackle affair, and I dare say he was right.'

'I would not have missed it for the world,' protested Caroline. 'A most extraordinary outcome to the mystery! And I cannot help liking that little Ada and her Gilbert, in spite of all the trouble they have caused. What will happen to them now?'

'They are to be married by special licence before they sail, and with the blessing of her family. I took her to

Mount Street yesterday, and there was a positive orgy of hugging and kissing and shrieks of delight. She did not appear to hate any of them very much.'

'*You* took her?'

'Well, I did not see who else was going to do so, and I felt she ought to be reconciled to her mother and Hester.'

'Do you think they deserved so much consideration?' enquired Caroline doubtfully. 'I do not presume to judge any woman for the way she lives her own life, but one who deliberately corrupts the innocence of a daughter or a younger sister—it seems to me that such a person must be utterly depraved!'

'The Gaineys are not depraved,' said Francis. 'They are, like most of us, so much the slaves of their own circumstances that any break with custom is held to be totally unacceptable. They simply wanted what they supposed was best for Ada, and although they are certainly not models of female propriety, they have a great deal of family affection.'

Caroline thought how much genuine kindness and generosity there was behind his sometimes odd behaviour and abrupt manner. He had made her feel ashamed of being so censorious. A short silence fell between them. She had heard all he had come to say. Soon he would get up and leave, and then the world would be grey indeed.

'How is Lord Eltham?' she asked. 'I am afraid he must be very unhappy.'

'Yes, he is. Poor Jack. He will get over it, however.' Francis paused, and then said: 'Don't set that down as one of my exhibitions of heartless indifference. I really do mean it. Jack will recover because he has a naturally good disposition that will save him from self-pity and all the grudges and torments of wounded pride. I never thought much of his abilities until now, but I know he is behaving far better than I did in a similar situation.'

The allusion was unmistakable.

'You are speaking of your engagement to Lavinia,' she said. 'But I don't know why you should reproach yourself, considering how nobly you protected her reputation at the cost of your own.'

'I was anything but noble that day by the river, when I half killed Alfred Pyke. Did she tell you about that? It was a very ugly episode, and I'm not proud of it.' He sat scowling into the past. 'Now I can't even remember how it felt to be so angry. What a fool I was to run mad over Lavinia.'

'You would not have been happy together; you are not at all well suited.'

'Nothing would convince me of that at the time. . . . If only you had been a young woman of the same age, my dear, instead of a staring little girl in a sun-bonnet—then I must have known at once that I was going to love you better than your sister.'

'It is not very likely. There can be no comparison between us, and I don't see how anyone could prefer—could have done, that is, when we were the same age. I mean, if we ever had been. Could you?' finished Caroline, in a piteous state of grammatical and emotional confusion.

'I'm sure I could,' said Francis, 'but this is hardly the moment for abstract speculation.'

They had been sitting decorously at opposite ends of Lavinia's new sofa. He leant across and took both her hands. Then he kissed her mouth. Caroline slipped into his arms as to the manner born. Nothing had ever come to her more naturally than knowing how to respond to Francis making love to her.

Presently he said, 'How old are you, Caroline?'

'Twenty-four.'

'And I am forty-one. Can you contemplate having a husband seventeen years older than yourself?'

'There does not seem to be such a great difference between us. And it will get narrower, won't it, as we grow older?'

'So it will. How wise you are. There is a stronger objection. Can you face life with a man who is so generally disliked that most of his acquaintances and even his own family are ready to brand him as a murderer?'

'Now you are talking nonsense,' she said briskly, for she sensed that this experience had shaken him a good deal. 'All these Gothic ideas were fostered artificially by the mystery of Ada's disappearance. Someone had to be the scapegoat, and I think they chose you because they don't understand you, are a little afraid of you, perhaps. You are cleverer than most of them.'

'And you may as well add that I have given offence by too much plain speaking,' said Francis with unusual humility.

'And perhaps by too much unplain speaking.'

'What do you mean by that?'

'Your frequent bouts of teasing: telling poor Miss Weatherby that you meant to cut down all the trees in the Wilderness, just to see if she would believe you. Or creeping stealthily out of the mausoleum like a stage villain, because you knew there was an inquisitive female gaping at you like a half-wit. The temptation must have been irresistible. But since you are in the habit of saying and doing such things with a perfectly straight face, you cannot complain when simple-minded people credit you with an occasional exploit you never even thought of.'

'Such as murder? Good God! Perhaps you think I ought to be flattered!'

She noticed with affectionate amusement that he was rather relieved by this explanation, but not in the least abashed.

'People are so literal,' he said. 'And so solemn. It's the bubble of solemnity I cannot help pricking. That may sound frivolous, yet the first useful thing I ever learnt in life was how to laugh—at myself for a start.'

'Who taught you that, Francis?'

'My father. He was a splendid fellow, very handsome and excelled in every kind of sport—what we should now-adays call a buck. My brother Dillingford—Jack's father —took after him. I was a puny creature, it was confidently predicted that they would never rear me, and my mother did her best to cosset me and turn me into a milksop, I was always poor little Frank to her. My father would have none of this. He teased me, sometimes spoke roughly to me, treated me like a real boy, instead of a freakish little candidate for an edifying deathbed. Needless to say, I always wanted to tag along after him and Dill. They never condescended to me, nor did they pretend to ignore my disadvantages, which would have been worse. My small stature was taken as a matter of course, and my father called me his powder-monkey. I have no doubt there were plenty of good souls who thought this was an unfeeling way to manage a sickly child, but he made a man of me and I always knew instinctively that he loved me as much as Dill.'

Caroline remembered Mrs. Harper's description of Francis as a child, and reflected how easy it was for even the most sensible person to be wrong. Her heart warmed towards two members of the Aubrey family whom she would never meet.

'I wish I had known your father and Dillingford. Does Jack resemble them at all?'

'In looks? Yes, a good deal. In character he belongs to the other side of the family; I suppose that has been half the trouble. Poor Dill made a fool of himself after he came into the title, and ran up a prodigious number of debts; when he was dying he wanted to make sure that his boy wouldn't fall into the same snares so he tied up everything in his will, and begged me to take good care of Jack. And I am afraid I have not carried out that commission as I ought. I have restored the family fortunes, I have even induced Jack to practise frugality. After all, he did set up a fashionable courtesan in a country cottage, and you can't be much more frugal than that! But we have never reached a proper understanding. He has been obliged to listen to a great deal of my plain speaking, and what you call my unplain speaking, and now I come to think of it, I don't suppose he ever had the faintest idea which was which.'

'I believe you will both manage better now,' Caroline consoled him.

Families were very odd, she decided, thinking not only of the Aubreys but also of the Gaineys, bullying Ada into a life that most women were advised to shun, and all from the most loving motives. And of Octavius Barrow, such an ill-adapted fledgling in the clerical nest. When you came to in-laws, the chances of not quite suiting each others' style were even greater. She said as much to Francis.

'I am sure Arthur will be thankful to be rid of me. I hope Lavinia won't mind too much.'

'I think she is resigned to the inevitable.'

'What do you—good gracious!' exclaimed Caroline.

'When she went off and left us alone together, it did not strike me at the time because I was so pleased to see you, but it was a very odd thing to do; do you think she guessed that you had come here to make me an offer?'

'Of course she did. And what's more, she told me it was now or never, because she couldn't go on conniving at my secret visits.'

'Well, I call that extremely mortifying.'

'You need not,' he assured her kindly. 'A little match-making is quite permissible. No one can say I was caught.'

'It would serve you right if they did,' said Caroline, refusing to be drawn. 'When I say I feel mortified, I mean that I have always considered myself so much quicker than Lavinia. How did she *know*?'

'The Lavinias of this world always know that sort of thing. You, my treasure, know a great many other things of more general interest . . . Now I suppose I shall have to request an interview of the worthy Arthur; not that we need his permission, but you would like everything settled in a friendly way.'

'Oh yes, for Lavinia's sake. We must try to convince him, without implicating her, that you are a proper person for me to marry.'

'Modify my black sheepishness? It seems rather a pity,' said Francis with a gleam in his eye that Caroline immediately distrusted.

'Francis! You are not to start teasing my brother-in-law, I won't have it.'

'Certainly not, if you don't wish me to do so. I merely said it seemed a pity, and if you were honest you would agree with me. He is a pompous windbag and you know it.'

'Perhaps,' she admitted, 'but he has been very good in

giving me a home all these years. I owe him a debt of gratitude.'

'Gratitude! That's a most pernicious sentiment, a famous breeder of insincerity. I hope you don't intend to be grateful to me, my girl!'

'No, why should I?' retorted Caroline instantly. 'For I can see I am going to be kept continually occupied in rescuing you from the awkward situations you have talked yourself into, and smoothing down all the feathers you have ruffled. Any gratitude will have to come from you.'

Francis began to laugh. 'My lovely Caroline—at last I have found a woman who can speak my language without needing an interpreter! How happy we are going to be!'